LEE COUNTY LIBRARY
SANFORD, N. C.

D1528279

Hangman's Springs

Also by John Reese

SURE SHOT SHAPIRO
THE LOOTERS
SUNBLIND RANGE
PITY US ALL
SINGALEE
HORSES, HONOR AND WOMEN
JESUS ON HORSEBACK: THE MOONEY COUNTY SAGA
ANGEL RANGE
THE BLOWHOLERS
THE LAND BARON
BIG HITCH
SPRINGFIELD .45–70
WEAPON HEAVY
THEY DON'T SHOOT COWARDS
THE SHARPSHOOTER
TEXAS GOLD
WES HARDIN'S GUN
A SHERIFF FOR ALL THE PEOPLE
BLACKSNAKE MAN

LEE COUNTY LIBRARY
SANFORD, N. C.

Hangman's Springs

JOHN REESE

DOUBLEDAY & COMPANY, INC.

GARDEN CITY, NEW YORK

1976

All of the characters in this book are fictitious,
and any resemblance to actual persons, living or
dead, is purely coincidental.

Library of Congress Cataloging in Publication Data

Reese, John Henry.
Hangman's springs.

I. Title.
PZ3.R25673Han   [PS3568.E43]   813'.5'4

ISBN: 0-385-12150-4
Library of Congress Catalog Card Number: 76-3930

Copyright © 1976 by John Reese
All Rights Reserved
Printed in the United States of America
First Edition

For George Flowers, fine writer, demanding critic, professional in all but his friendship.

Hangman's Springs

CHAPTER ONE

A brief rattle of gunfire from the foothills to the south-east. Jefferson Hewitt, holding his borrowed brown stallion down to the slow gait of the loaded carriage, went rigid in the saddle. The sudden acceleration of pulse and breathing warned him of the need for self-control, to keep from alarming the people in the carriage. He could feel the cords in his throat pulling against the skin as his mouth pulled down, taut.

The Mexican coachman on the high box turned and rolled his eyes wildly at Hewitt. Little sounds—the creaking of saddles, low mutterings, the jingle of bit-rings—told him that the ten armed men riding behind the carriage had also heard the gunshots.

He shook his head sternly at the coachman, and turned in the saddle to catch the eye of Nicolas, who commanded the ten-man guard. Nicolas was only a kid, no more than seventeen, but he was hard to stampede. Nicolas merely nodded his head slightly. It was his way of saying, "We heard it. Don't worry, we're not frightened."

The carriage was a fine one, but it must have been insufferably hot in it. The air was full of *jijenes*, vicious little sandflies that would be with them until, one could hope, a breeze came up. On a horse, a man had a chance against them. In the carriage, you were trapped.

"Jeff!"

It was the girl, Josefina, who rode in the front seat of the carriage, facing backward. Hewitt spurred Coco, the bullheaded brown stallion, a little closer, to lean out of the saddle.

"Yes?" he said.

"That was shooting, wasn't it?"

No use lying to her. "Sure was."

"They're catching up—the *rurales*, I mean, aren't they?"

She was almost homely, with that tense, angry frown on her olive face. Only in repose was Josefina an attractive girl, and he had seldom seen her in repose during the three weeks he had known her.

"Now, Josefina," he said, "if you know that they're rurales, you know more than I do."

"You make me so *damn* mad," she said. "How much farther is it to the springs?"

"Twelve, fifteen miles. I'm not sure."

"Can't we make a run for it?"

"We'd only kill the horses and never get there, in this heat." He gave her, deliberately, a fatherly smile as he switched to Spanish: "*Cálmate, cálmate, chiquitina. Por qué está tan nerviosa? Yo estoy!*"

"Oh, *crap*," she said, to show him what she thought of his Spanish.

He grinned and let the carriage move ahead a little. Calm yourself, calm yourself, little one. Why are you so nervous? I am here! That would keep her blood pressure up, and her nerve along with it, for a while.

Hewitt knew that his short-sleeved white shirt made him a conspicuous target, but it was the coolest thing he had, and he believed devoutly that the horse did not live that could outrun Coco. The stallion was only four years old, only half broken. He was a big horse with powerful legs and fine, shod feet, and was in perfect condition at about eleven hundred pounds.

He turned in the saddle to face east, tipping the wide brim of his hat down over his face to shade his eyes. He was not sure, but he thought he saw the cloud of dust raised by the horse herd, and he did not like it. When they had left the *rancho*, at about three this morning, there had been one hundred and five fine horses in that herd. He knew that they had picked up several more on the trail so far.

Those horses would be worth at least one hundred dollars each, once they were across the Rio Grande and in the United States. That meant that better than ten thousand dollars was hidden in that cloud of dust—and they should have been farther from this coach road and closer to the foothills.

Hewitt pulled Coco aside and rode him far away from the carriage, into complete silence except for the infuriating, endless whine of the jijenes. He could not be sure he saw anything, now. The humid heat-haze distorted even the foothills.

Again he went tense in the saddle as a single gunshot sounded. He listened a moment longer and heard nothing. He turned the horse and cantered him back to the carriage.

The owner of the carriage, the horses, and the rancho from which they came leaned out. "That one was a rifle," he said, "wasn't it?"

"Had to be," Hewitt said curtly.

Don Aristide Castañeda López took out a fresh cambric

handkerchief to pat the sweat from his face. There was no expression on it, and none in his eyes.

"Tell Nicolas," he said, "to take a couple of men and look into it. We'll meet them at the *charco*. I want them to ride somewhere between the horses and ourselves, observing and, when necessary, reporting."

"I'll go myself," Hewitt said.

Aristide smiled. "In this heat?" he said. "Nonsense! Take it easy. That's an order, Jeff."

"God damn it," Hewitt said, "I'm giving the orders now, remember? I'll see if I can find Mose Kirk and send him back to ride with you."

"You drive a hard bargain."

"Yes, and live up to it, too."

Coco wanted to run, and here there was room for it. Once this alluvial plain had been the greatest grove of piñon pines in the world. They had all been cut off, a century or two ago, to make charcoal to smelt gold and silver for the Spanish kings and queens. Now nothing grew here except creosote bush, sagebrush, and an occasional cactus in the thin, wiry grass.

When he spotted the horse herd, he was no more than five or six miles from the coach road and a dozen miles from the foothills. The Americans of whom Aristide was so proud—his *guardia gringo*—were having trouble with the nervous horses. Hewitt spotted one of the men and stood up in the stirrups to wave his hat.

The American saw him and waved back. He put his horse into a run to meet Hewitt. It was George Boney, the foreman of the five men and the one Hewitt liked least.

"You heered the firin'?" was Boney's greeting.

"Hell, yes. What was it?"

"Them damn policemen, I reckon."

"Who fired first?"

"You be damn sure," Boney said stridently, "that I ain't settin' there like a stump and lettin' them git close enough to pick me off. *We* fired first, and you—"

"Who fired the rifle?" Hewitt cut in.

"Orval did. I told him to keep them—"

"Where did he get the rifle?" Hewitt snarled. "From a dead rural, didn't he? God damn you, Boney, answer me!"

"Nobody talks to me like that!"

Hewitt dug his heels into Coco's sides and slammed the big stud into Boney's mount. There was no such thing as a bad horse on the Castañeda place, but neither was there one that could stand against the brown stallion.

Boney's terrified gelding fell back on its haunches. Coco wanted to fight. Hewitt had to haul back on the stern curb bit, and then the horse went up on its hind legs instead of backing out of contact with the gelding. Boney screamed and tumbled out of the saddle.

Hewitt snatched off his hat and leaned forward to slap it down over the stallion's head. Coco came down, and Hewitt tumbled out of the saddle, holding the reins in his right hand while he clutched the reins of Boney's horse with his left. The stallion was still in a mood to kill, but that hat over his eyes had confused him briefly. Hewitt pressed him back with short, sharp tugs on the reins.

"Behave, sir! Stand, now. Stand, I said!"

The stallion stood. Boney pulled himself to his feet a safe distance from both horses and began to slap the dust out of his clothing. He was a wiry, hatchet-faced man in his late forties, with a month's growth of curly, red-brown beard covering a receding chin.

"You shore can handle that Coco horse," he said with reluctant admiration. "I'd-a bet nobody on earth could make that outlaw toe the line the way you done, Mr. Hewitt."

"If he works for me," said Hewitt, "he toes the line, Boney, and don't you ever forget it. Now tell me what happened."

The other Americans had managed to bring the horse herd to a halt no more than a mile away. They had had their run—in this heat, not a long one—and would be easier to manage for a while.

"They's three of them," Boney said, "and they's all three got ca'tridge bandoliers crisscrossed over their chests, and brand-new hats. Now, that spells rurales to me, and anytime you meet the rurales, they're lookin' for horses. The crowbaits they was ridin', they couldn't even whup them into a run."

The rurales were the country policemen that President Porfirio Díaz had organized to reduce banditry throughout Mexico. Most of them had been bandits themselves—and this was not necessarily a moral judgment on them. Ever since the collapse of the French imperial occupation and the endless revolutions that followed it, disorder had been the norm throughout Mexico. Had President Juárez lived—

But he had not. The one man strong enough to rule the country and just enough to inspire its people had been found dead at his desk one morning. Now another strong man had attained the presidency, and was swiftly restoring order to his poor, tortured country. Whether he was just enough to deserve his countrymen's trust remained to be seen.

Don Aristide Castañeda López thought not. Aristide was an educated man, and an opinionated one. He had been educated in the United States and France—and to Porfirio Díaz, anything French was suspect. The last time

Aristide had seen the President, they had had a polite little quarrel. That was less than a year ago.

Now Aristide had turned his enormous landholdings over to a cousin to run for him, the cousin being a loyal *porfirista* who could stave off total ruin, if anyone could. Aristide was moving his entire family to the United States, and from there, possibly, to Europe. There was no problem of money. He had admitted to Hewitt that he did not know how much he had.

The trouble was that he had waited too long to make up his mind to leave, despite the warnings of his cousin that eventually the President would get around to him. Therefore, he had sent for Hewitt to get him out of his own country, family and all.

The final idiocy, Hewitt thought, was taking so many of his best horses with him, just to spite the President and his rurales. What did ten thousand dollars mean to a man with Aristide's wealth? The horses, on the other hand, would have been a noble peace offering. God knew the rurales needed them; and as Hewitt himself had pointed out to Aristide, "It's your country, too, man. Let them have the horses!"

Aristide had refused. Now, apparently, the rurales had tried to take them, and the damned riffraff Americans that Aristide had hired had precipitated a brief but murderous gunfight. One of the rurales had been shot from the saddle, and his worthless horse captured for the sake of the big Mauser rifle lashed to its saddle. The other two rurales had doggedly followed the horse herd—at least until someone took a shot at them with the captured rifle.

"Who did the shooting?" Hewitt demanded.

"Which shootin', the six-gun or rifle?" Boney countered.

Hewitt let go of Boney's horse and smashed the back of

his hand across Boney's mouth. He shifted hands quickly, taking Coco's reins in his left. He dropped his right to the .45 he wore in a holster he had designed himself. It clipped to the belt that supported his pants and lay almost horizontally across his belly. A twist freed it from the spring-loaded pawl that gripped the front sight and held it in place.

He had the .45 in his hand before Boney could get his hand on his own gun. "Go ahead," he said, "try your luck."

Boney's hand came away quickly from his gun. "You shore are tetchy, Mr. Hewitt," he said.

"It's the heat," said Hewitt. "One more time: who did the shooting? Start at the beginning."

"Well," said Boney, "it was like this . . ."

CHAPTER TWO

The three riders with their new, peaked hats and their overloaded bandoliers had come up behind the horse herd no more than an hour ago. Plainly, they had been trailing it since early morning. They surely were tired, hungry, and desperate at the thought of so many fine horses getting away. On the worn-out horses they rode, only desperate men would have attacked against odds of five to three.

Boney had been riding between the foothills and the herd. He looked back from a slight elevation and saw the three. Blackie Randall was tailing the herd. Boney spun his horse and dug in his spurs.

Blackie saw him coming, looked back over his shoulder, and saw the three rurales. Boney waved and pointed for Blackie to leave the horse herd and ride west, and Blackie had sense enough to seek what cover there was. When Boney rode straight for the rurales, Blackie Randall came up on their flank. They did not see him.

Boney held up his hand, palm outward, a sign that said, clearly, *Stop—keep your distance!* The trouble with it was that the Mexican police, not hired American thugs, gave the orders in Mexico. The three came straight on.

Blackie Randall carried two .45 Colts, and he had a

horse he could handle with his knees. He drew both guns and came in firing. The three rurales, startled, turned to face him.

Boney counted Blackie's shots. When there had been ten, leaving only one in each of Blackie's guns, Boney opened up with his own. The distance was closing rapidly. The Mexicans were not outgunned, but the inferiority of their horses was a fatal handicap. They had waited too long to retreat safely, yet they tried to retreat.

Blackie brought down one of them with his eleventh shot. It was the man with the Mauser. Both policemen tried to beat him to the dead man's horse, but when it bolted it ran away from them and toward Blackie. Once he had the rifle, it was no longer an even fight. There was nothing the Mexicans could do but retreat.

That was the gunfire that had first put Hewitt's nerves on edge. Still, the two survivors hung doggedly on the trail of the magnificent horse herd. Blackie saw his chance to take cover in a dry ravine. He dismounted, tied his horse, and waited with the rifle.

"Only then he missed," Boney said disgustedly. "Them goddamn little flies was drivin' him bughouse. At least he learned them not to foller too damn close."

Well, the damage was done. "All right," Hewitt said, "you fools get the herd moving again, but I want Mose Kirk to ride with the carriage for a while. That's the first thing I want you to do—send him to take my place."

"Why Mose?"

"Someday," Hewitt said wearily, "maybe you'll learn that when I give an order, you don't stop to discuss it with me—you just jump. Go get Mose, and both of you get the hell back here on the double."

Boney's horse had run only a little way and he came back at Boney's whistle. "Everything I say," Boney said as he swung up into the saddle, "is the wrong thing today, looks like. I don't mean to rile you, Mr. Hewitt."

"Then don't."

Hewitt waited, fighting jijenes. In a moment, the two came loping their horses toward him. The horses in the herd had rested a moment. They had back their wind and their curiosity, and they followed Boney and Mose Kirk until they were within a few hundred yards of Hewitt.

The Kirk kid was not impressive, but he was the pick of the five Americans, to Hewitt's mind. He was surely no more than seventeen or eighteen, one of those woebegone, meek, and usually silent boys who seemed never to have had a home of any kind. His pink cheeks were covered with a pale down that had never been touched by the barber's blade. His blue eyes stared out at the world with a look of pain, from under pale lashes. His curly yellow hair sprang out in all directions from under his old, torn hat.

The thing that made him the man to send back to ride with the carriage was not his lost-dog decency, but his dumb, worshipful adoration of Josefina Castañeda. Mose probably did not even know he was in love with the girl. But Hewitt did. Another thing—Mose spoke Spanish, not well, but enough to get by.

"Mose," Hewitt said, "I want you to go back and ride with the carriage, as close to it as you can get without getting into it, understand?"

"Yes, Mr. Hewitt," Kirk said, his face lighting up with pleasure at the prospect of seeing Josefina again.

"You're in charge. Don't hesitate to overrule Don Aristide if you have to. Nicolas and his men will obey you. The main thing I'm worried about is troops. If you see anything that looks like a column of cavalry coming toward you from the north, tell Nicolas to send men a-helling to bring me. Got that?"

"Yes, sir."

"The carriage is not to stop. Neither is it to try to make a run for it. You've got to spare those horses! The family has plenty of food. See that they eat on the move. Don Aristide will want to stop and have a picnic somewhere. To hell with that!"

Kirk was nodding solemnly, almost overcome with his responsibilities. "I won't let 'em," he said. "Where will you be?"

"I'm going to try," Hewitt said, "to talk with those rurales. Make a deal with them for part of the horse herd. But you don't need to tell Don Aristide that."

"No, Mr. Hewitt, I won't. I just wanted to know where Nico would look for you."

"Hell, Mr. Hewitt, have you gone plumb crazy?" said Boney. "How are you going to palaver with them damn policemen?"

"I don't know," said Hewitt, "since you have killed one of their comrades. But I would rather dicker with two of them than a dozen. You don't think those three were the only ones around, do you?"

Boney could only gape at him. Hewitt went on savagely, "They were only trying to keep you in sight while a fourth man that you didn't see went to bring up the main strength. You had flat orders to notify me the moment you saw or heard anything suspicious. Instead, you and that fool, Blackie Randall, had to make it a killing case. Now do you see what you have done?"

"Well, hell, Mr. Hewitt—"

"When I came across," Hewitt interrupted him, "there were two squadrons of cavalry and two companies of infantry at Reynosa. I heard there were twice that many at Matamoros, and it would be strange if there weren't.

"We've got to find a place somewhere between Reynosa and Matamoros where we can get a loaded carriage across the Rio Grande during the rainy season, and slip all those horses over at the same time. We've got to time it to approach the river at night, but now you've blown our timing all to hell—now you've got the rurales on our tails, madder than wasps. How many horses have you got now, do you know?"

"The last count," said the crestfallen Boney, "they was a hundred and sixteen. Some of 'em ain't the best horses in the world, but we picked up some real good ones, too."

"You won't pick up any more," Hewitt said. "Get them out on the coach road ahead of the carriage and go like hell for Charco Verdugo. Tire them out, and they'll be easy to hold around water, and you can get them all watered before we get there with the carriage. You know what to look for?"

"I never been over that trail afore, but Dugan Peeke has."

"'Charco Verdugo' is the Spanish name for Hangman's Springs—or pond or waterhole or whatever. You'll be able to see five big cottonwoods from quite a distance. Make sure it's five! You'll see other clumps of cottonwoods, but there's not water enough at any of them and they're far out of our way. You've made your last mistake, Boney. Make one more and I'll have your hide."

"I'll git there," Boney promised, "with the herd. Then all I do is wait there fer you?"

"Yes."

"How about feed fer the horses?"

"You can let them forage a little way, but keep that herd under control! Do you realize what we're trying to do? We're trying to steal ten thousand dollars' worth of horses right out from under the Mexican government's nose, because that's what Don Aristide wants to do. And you don't get paid until we're across the Rio—clear?"

"I swear to God, Mr. Hewitt—"

"On your way, both of you!"

They rode off in their separate directions, Mose Kirk to catch up with the carriage, happily; George Boney to get the herd on the trail again, apprehensively. Hewitt waited until the horses were on the move and the dust they left behind had settled.

Then, keeping under cover wherever he could, he made his way on Coco toward the rising elevations below the foothills. Not until he was alone did he realize how hungry he was. It was long past noon, and the last food he had eaten was shortly after daylight. He had declined to eat with the family in the carriage. Instead, he had shared the *burritos*—wheat-flour *tortillas* rolled around fried beans that have been ˙spiced with chili—with young Nicolas and his men.

Now he drooled at the thought of the roasted chickens, the fresh, brown, whole-wheat bread baked by the wife of Don Aristide herself, and the other goodies in the linen-covered hampers that took up most of the space in the center of the carriage.

But Jefferson Hewitt had been hungrier than this, hotter than this, and angrier than this, many a time in his life. Born in an Ozark cabin a little more than forty years ago, he had been barely able to sign his name when he lied about his age to join the Army. Five years later, he was a corporal and the company clerk of Headquarters Company at the Presidio of San Francisco—some officers said the best company clerk in the Army.

He was also, by then, well on his way to becoming an

educated man. He envied the officers their privileges of rank not at all, but he did envy them their knowledge, and he set about acquiring it voraciously. He left the Army after giving information against dishonest and incompetent officers, in one of those quiet proceedings that never came to court-martial. The officers were permitted to resign with their reputations—and their privileges—intact.

He took the first job he could get, as a detective with the Pinkerton Agency on the Oakland docks, where he quickly broke a robbery ring that had been stealing shippers blind. He worked for the Pinkertons several years, building a reputation as a crafty, indeed highly intellectual operative with a gift of command and no fear of making decisions. He had always been a good shot. In the Army he became a better one. As a Pinkerton detective, his reputation with either short or long gun became a legend. Hewitt saw to it, with continual practice, that he was almost as good as his reputation.

He quit his job when a Cheyenne bank and a man in a surety-bonding company offered to back him. The man was a German immigrant and also an intellectual of sorts. But where all of Hewitt's knowledge had been acquired in lonely study, Conrad Meuse had attended the best universities in Germany, and had taught in one. There, he had made himself objectionable to imperial authorities, to the point where it became far healthier for him to seek a new life in the New World.

Conrad was, among other things, a fine accountant and economist. The West was growing faster than the surety companies of the East could keep up with. There was a real need for Bankers Bonding and Indemnity Company, as the partnership came to be called. Conrad remained in Cheyenne, ran the office, and wrote the bonds. Hewitt

made the field investigations for them—and also for any
other paying clients who needed B.B. and I.'s services.

Hewitt and Meuse made a good team. Both were bachelors, and both were acquisitive, individualistic, and self-confident to a fault. They could not stand each other's
company for very long at a time, yet Hewitt had an abiding and deep affection for his partner, and he knew that
Conrad held him to be the only real friend he had ever
had. Conrad had invested Hewitt's money so brilliantly
that he was now a rich man.

He could have retired and lived in security the rest of
his life, but, like Conrad, he was driven by the desire to
be still wealthier, as well as by a restlessness that would
not let him remain idle for long.

The entire West was Hewitt's beat. He got back to
Cheyenne two or three times a year, at most. The rest of
the time, the partners kept in touch by wire—their telegraph bills were shocking, especially to Conrad.

For the present, Hewitt was cut off from his home
office entirely. The wires were down in this part of Mexico, and the closest telegraph office was across the border
in Texas. And if there ever had been a time when he
wanted to give Conrad a few choice, pointed words of advice, it was now.

For this job of helping Aristide Castañeda López and
his family escape from Mexico until President Díaz
cooled off had been Conrad's deal from the first. Hewitt
could still recall, word for word, the last hortatory wire he
had had from Conrad. He had already rejected the job
twice when he got the telegram, which he could still
recite:

UNABLE UNDERSTAND ATTITUDE STOP RICH FEE LEAST OF
ATTRACTIONS STOP CLIENT PLEASANT CULTIVATED GEN-

TLEMAN OF WIT AND WISDOM AND FAMILY A DELIGHT
STOP YOUR EXPENSE ACCOUNT OKLA JOB OUTRAGEOUS
STOP NOT EVEN GOOD FICTION STOP CLEARLY YOUR
NERVES NEED REST AND MEXICO CONTRACT PERFECT
VACATION STOP WHICH PREFER SERVE THIS CLIENT OR
EXPLAIN NINE HUNDRED DOLLARS OKLA OVERCHARGE.

Ah, yes indeed, a perfect vacation spot this part of
Mexico was, in August! But Conrad was a demon on expense accounts and Hewitt had been just too tired to
argue with him. He wished now that he had.

CHAPTER THREE

Holding Coco to a walk, Hewitt cautiously climbed the slanting, gullied *mesa*. A half-hour's surveillance convinced him that the two surviving rurales were not on the trail of the horse herd—and why should they be? It would take no great tracking skill to follow that trail, and anyone who knew the country would know they were heading for Charco Verdugo anyway.

Nowhere else was there water enough for this herd. Hewitt gave Coco his head, and the big brown stud made a beeline for the carriage. When it first came into sight, Hewitt felt a swift surge of apprehension. The carriage was stopped near a dusty tree. Aristide and his family had taken shelter in the sparse shade of the tree. Around the carriage itself was noise, commotion, and a cloud of dust.

They were changing carriage teams, and the fresh horses could only have come out of the horse herd as it passed them. Mose Kirk was completely in charge. Nicolas and his men were swiftly unharnessing weary horses and throwing the harness onto fresh ones.

"Kind of risky business, isn't it?" Hewitt said, pulling Coco up beside Kirk's horse.

The youth gave him that look that was innocence or stupidity or both. "What is?"

"Trying to break four wild horses to harness," Hewitt said, "with women and children in the carriage."

"Oh, shoot, Mr. Hewitt, these ain't wild. These four have all been worked in harness," Kirk said.

All of Aristide's horses were blacks, browns, and dark bays. The four being harnessed might be somewhat heavier-boned than the average, but it took an expert to see it—and something more than an expert to have picked them out of more than a hundred other horses.

His respect for Mose Kirk increased immensely. The four fresh horses were not exactly tame, but if Kirk said they could be worked on the carriage, they could. Hewitt dismounted and led Coco over to where Aristide and his family stood disconsolately under the dusty tree, fanning away the persistent jijenes.

"You think it was necessary to change teams, my friend Hewitt?" Aristide said.

"Maybe not necessary," said Hewitt, "but smart. It's still a long old ride, and why kill willing horses when you've got remounts?"

"I suppose so," said Aristide, "but nothing seems to go well today, does it?"

"The day isn't over yet."

"That's rather cryptic. What does it mean?"

"It means," Hewitt said, "that things could get worse before they get better. Your man Blackie Randall killed one of the rurales."

"I know. Regrettable, but necessary."

"It was not necessary, but I'll tell you what could become necessary before this day is over."

"What?"

"We may have to part with some horses—probably half of them, perhaps all of them—to get you and your family across the river."

"Please, Jeff, do not unnecessarily frighten my family," Aristide said. "Nothing moves swiftly or promptly in Mexico. Rather, we do, but we are the exception. Long before my enemies can organize against us, you will have us across the river. I am sure of that."

"I wish I were," Hewitt said. "We've got the rurales behind us, and kill one of them and you're automatically an outlaw. We've got troops ahead of us, including some cavalry. Feed must be getting short around Reynosa and Matamoros. We could run into forage parties anywhere, anytime."

"Not in this heat, friend Hewitt. No soldier will venture far from the *cantinas* and the beer. If we do meet a forage party, we'll surely have it outnumbered, and a handful of gold coins—"

"Will only make them want more," Hewitt cut in. "I'm going to make the best deal I can with horses. That's the one advantage we have—horses to spare."

"No, these porfiristas get none of my fine horses. I forbid that, Jeff."

"Then," said Hewitt, "you get your family over the best you can. I'm heading for the border. I told you, I do things my way or I don't do them."

Aristide's wife laid her hand on her husband's arm, to silence him. "Aristide is upset," she said in her soft voice, "but he's a reasonable man and he has given his word. We will do things your way, Mr. Hewitt."

Hewitt looked at Aristide. "I hope we understand each other. I don't like the look of things a bit, and if I'm going to be responsible, I want a free hand."

"You have it, of course," Aristide said, patting his wife's hand. "Conrad said I would have to trust you, and that you are a stubborn, headstrong man who is usually right."

"Well," said Hewitt, smiling, "now and then I am."

It was hard not to like Aristide. It was impossible to dislike his wife, Helen. She was his second wife, a very fair, gentle woman of about twenty-four. Her father, Hewitt understood, owned a small business of some kind in Washington, D.C. One of the background reasons for their return to the United States was that Helen was expecting a baby in the late fall, and both she and Aristide wished it to be born in the United States.

It seemed to Hewitt to be a real love match, despite the fact that Aristide was almost twice his wife's age. It was hard to say which would be the most helpless in an emergency. Aristide looked tough. He was a burly, swarthy man with the stern, big-featured face of the stone idols found whenever new Aztec ruins were excavated. If there was a drop of European blood in him, it did not show.

Yet he had been the only boy in a big family, and had been indulged since babyhood as only the heir of a rich Mexican family could be indulged. He had a Harvard degree and one from Cambridge. His English, while sometimes stilted, was better than Hewitt's. He spoke perfect French and adequate German. Hewitt could get by in French, but the German he spoke was a Hessian Plattdeutsch dialect that horrified Conrad and amused Aristide.

The world was full of people like Aristide, dreamers who never quite connected with reality. The lucky ones were the ones who had money. Those without it went down early and often violently in the confrontation with life as it was, not as they had dreamed it to be.

If Aristide had charm and a certain childish innocence under that Aztec exterior, his daughter was another proposition altogether. Josefina was the child of his first wife, who had died so young that Josefina could not remember her. She had been brought up by a series of *nanas* and governesses in America, England, and France, and was at least as well-educated as Aristide.

In most respects, Josefina was far more Mexican than Aristide was, although she had seen very little of her own country. In one vital respect, however, she was as alien as she could be. Never in God's world would Josefina be content to be the conventional Mexican wife. She was outspoken, bossy, often vulgar—and, Hewitt was sure, anything but innocent about the opposite sex.

Her unfailingly courteous attitude toward Helen was puzzling. Hewitt thought that probably Aristide and his daughter had had this out long ago, the father having his way. Usually it was an icy courtesy, proving only that Josefina could be as pliable as spring steel *when she had to be.*

On the other hand, Hewitt had also detected signs of real warmth between the woman and the girl. In his brief stay at the rancho before they started this idiot flight to the border, he had seen them talking together with an intimacy that could not be mistaken. Rather, the daughter had been talking—swiftly, passionately, pouring out her heart about something. Helen had listened, her pretty face alight with compassion and interest. The few such scenes had suggested to Hewitt that Josefina might never before have had a real woman friend.

She was a strange one, contentious, more than a little bitter, and too outspoken for her own good. She could have been a very pretty girl, Hewitt thought, if only she had been able to relax and laugh.

Hewitt watched approvingly as the four new horses were hitched to the carriage. Mose Kirk could get his way with men with a minimum of orders—a good sign. The horses danced restlessly in the traces as the coachman sorted out the long lines in his hands.

"I reckon," Kirk said, "the family ort to load up and git goin', don't you?"

"Aren't you going to run some of the ginger out of the teams before you risk the ladies?" Hewitt asked.

Those blue eyes were full of puzzlement. "Why? He kin handle 'em. If we have to run fer it, they kin use all the ginger they got."

"You think we might have to run for it?"

Kirk merely nodded. Hewitt dismounted and handed Kirk the reins of his horse.

"Let's get on the road, please," he said.

He offered his hand to Helen, who got into the carriage and sank down in her seat, facing forward. When he gave his hand to Josefina, he happened to glance up at Kirk. The look on the kid's face made him wish that he had let him load up the family. To touch Josefina's hand would have made Kirk's whole day worthwhile.

There was a maid along, an elderly woman whose name was Socorro Campos. Aristide deferred to her, to her great confusion. Socorro clambered into the carriage without Hewitt's help and sat down beside Josefina, facing backward. Aristide got into the carriage last, and sat down beside his wife.

"Mose," Hewitt said, "stay close to those leaders for a few minutes, will you? Just to be sure."

The four horses felt the slack go out of the lines. The coachman chirped to them. There were a few seconds of confusion as the carriage was jerked into motion. Suddenly the four half-wild horses were a team. Hewitt mounted Coco and walked him along beside the carriage.

"Aristide," he said, "I think I'm going to make some changes right now."

"In what, friend Hewitt?"

"How much do you trust George Boney?"

Aristide smiled and held his thumb and forefinger about half an inch apart. "This far," he said, "while I have an eye on him, much less when I do not. Boney's value is not in his reliability, but in his toughness. He is a very dangerous man, and that's exactly why I hired him."

"And the others—Orval Honeycutt—Dugan Peeke—Blackie Randall?"

"They are Boney's men, not mine. Worthless but dangerous, except that Boney can handle them."

"How about Mose Kirk?"

"An aimless boy. Not bad, not good, not anything."

"Where did you get him?"

"Kirk? I saw him one evening in the shade of the trees, eating as though he had not eaten for weeks. All sorts come through, Jeff. I suppose he's in trouble of some kind in the States, but I felt sorry for him and told Boney to make him part of my guardia gringo."

Hewitt thought it over for a moment. "Well," he said, "I'm going to send Kirk on ahead to take charge of the horse herd. I'm going to relieve Boney of command."

Aristide frowned. "Why, Jeff? I have never seen any indication that Kirk can command anything."

"He's young and green," Hewitt said, "but he's serious, and he seems to get things done. He wouldn't have let that policeman be killed. If we run into troops, he won't lose his head. Boney will."

Plainly, Aristide did not agree, but he had become reconciled to letting Hewitt take charge. "As you like," he said. Suddenly he smiled. "It will please Josefina, at least. She has been very kind to young Kirk, poor lad."

"Do you know if Boney can read and write?"

Aristide frowned. "Let's see. Yes, I know he can. Why?"

"If you'll lend me some paper, I'm going to make it as

official as I can," Hewitt said grimly. "I'll want you to countersign the order, too."

"You have paper, Helen," Josefina said eagerly. "Lend Mr. Hewitt your letter paper, why don't you?"

Aristide's wife dug into a little leather case and handed Hewitt a pad of highly scented paper that had a pale pink cast. He dismounted, letting the carriage go on ahead, knelt, and used his knee for a desk. When he had finished writing, he caught up with the carriage and handed the pad to Aristide. The rich man frowned over the message and then signed it.

"Conrad," he said, handing it over, "is somewhat conservative, don't you agree?"

"In what way?"

"He described you as stubborn. Strong-minded. Ruthless. Unpredictable. Devious-minded and even sly. Now that I have come to know you, I regard that as understatement, friend Hewitt."

Hewitt grinned at him, took the note back, and spurred ahead to catch up with Kirk. The four carriage horses were behaving perfectly, moving out with a stride that would have made them worth a thousand dollars in any urban horse market in the United States. Kirk had an eye for a horse, whether he had anything else or not.

"Mose, can you read?"

"Sure. I read printin' easier than writin'," Kirk said laconically, "but I kin read both. Why?"

"Then read this."

Hewitt handed over the scented note. Kirk read it slowly, with a frown. It said:

To George Boney:

You are herewith relieved of command of the American crew and of the charge of the horse herd.

*Mose Kirk will command from the moment you re-
ceive this. I make this change because I expect trouble with either the troops, or the rurales, or both, and
I want Kirk to prevent as much of it as possible. I expect you, Honeycutt, Peeke, and Randall to take his
orders as you would mine. If you do so, there will be
a $100 bonus for each of you the moment we are
back on American soil.*

J. Hewitt

Approved, Aristide Castañeda L.

Eventually Kirk looked up. "George, he ain't goin' to
like this a bit," he said.

"Do you think he'll lead the others off?"

"No, they's all broke, so they cain't quit their jobs,"
Kirk said thoughtfully.

"He fancies himself with a gun," Hewitt suggested.

Kirk nodded. "Yes, but he ain't as tough as he thinks he
is. That don't worry me."

"Mose, are you a gunman yourself? A good one?"

The youth was silent for a moment, thinking over how
much he should say. "I reckon there's better," he said,
"but I ain't never met none."

"Ever kill a man?"

"Well, he called hisself that. Fer as I's concerned, he
was just a goddamned animal. Mr. Hewitt, you say you
expect trouble with the troops. What the *hell* kin I do if
the soldiers try to take them horses?"

"The best you can, Mose. Bluff it out. Offer them ten
horses—twenty—go to half the herd if you have to. Don't
let their uniforms frighten you. They pull those pants on
one leg at a time, the same as we do."

"My old bastard of a daddy was a soldier," Kirk said.

"Named me after his commander. John Singleton Mosby Kirk is my name. You ever hear of Mosby the Raider?"

"You bet I have, Mose," Hewitt said, grinning. "What we want to do now is stand off the raiders."

Kirk nodded, his serious look showing that he saw nothing to laugh at. He folded the note, stuffed it into his shirt pocket along with the little leather bag of Mexican tobacco and the soft inner cornshucks with which he rolled his cigarettes, and heeled his horse into a canter. He did not look back as he rode on to take over his new duties at Charco Verdugo.

And now Hewitt was sure that Aristide had been blind to something that could be important. Well, well, he thought, John Singleton Mosby Kirk and Josefina Castañeda Baca! There's a lot more to this kid than I saw at first, and Aristide overlooked it, too. But Josefina didn't. . . .

CHAPTER FOUR

About an hour later, a sluggish breeze sprang up from the
west. It was hot, and heavy with moisture from the Gulf.
It made things more difficult for human beings, and still
worse for horses.

Hewitt's white shirt, sweat-soaked, picked up so much
dust that it quickly turned gray. The two two-horse carriage teams dripped sweat, and there was lather around
their muzzles and wherever the harness chafed.

In the carriage, Aristide dozed, holding his wife's hand.
She must have been in misery, being so heavy with child,
but when she caught Hewitt's eye, she managed a small
smile. The maid, Socorro, seemed indifferent to everything. Hardship of all kinds was the heritage of the Indian peasant stock from which she had come. She would
survive this as her ancestors had survived everything.

Josefina alone seemed to be alert to what went on
around her. Hewitt had avoided her as much as possible
at the rancho. She could be real trouble, and he sensed
something unscrupulous in her that meant that the man
who got into trouble with her could expect no more compassion from her than from her family.

Now she seemed to seek his eyes, his thoughts, but not

to tempt him. We, her attitude seemed to say, have a se-
cret! Only you and I know about Mose Kirk. . . .

The intractable sun hung forever in the overhead sky,
refusing to descend. They plodded on.

"Señor," came the voice of young Nicolas, who commanded the armed guard behind the carriage.

At the same time, the maid, Socorro, made a small, gut-
tural sound in her throat. Hewitt, riding beside the carriage, saw her point toward the east. When he looked
back, Nicolas had stood up in the stirrups and was shad-
ing his eyes to look in the same direction.

"What's the matter?" Josefina asked.

Hewitt frowned and shook his head, but Socorro gave
it away. "*Soldados*," she said.

The carriage was between Hewitt and the soldiers. He
leaned down to take Aristide's sleeve and shake him
awake. "We're going to have visitors, Aristide," he said.
"Let me handle it. All of you just act bored."

The coachman had seen the soldiers, too. He did not
know whether to whip up the teams or stop. Hewitt told
him to ignore the soldiers and keep on at the same pace,
sparing his horses all he could.

He pulled Coco to a stop and let the carriage move on
ahead. The soldiers came into view, thirteen of them, apparently an officer and twelve men, all badly mounted.
The officer wore a huge sword—not a cavalry saber, but a
broadsword. Only three of them seemed to carry rifles—
not carbines, but heavy old Mausers.

"Be calm," he told Nicolas and his men as they walked
their horses past him. "We won't make a fight."

"*Sí, señor*," said Nicolas.

A heavy, old, two-wheeled cart pulled by two small,
sweating broncos came struggling up out of a ravine
behind the soldiers. Hewitt could see the officer turn to

bark orders. One man remained behind with the cart, which was being driven by a boy in short pants, with bare feet.

The other soldiers formed a wide line, with the officer in the center, and spurred their weary horses toward the carriage. As usual, Hewitt felt the old, familiar tingle of enjoyment that he supposed he would never outgrow. He did not enjoy fighting, but he did enjoy confrontations, crises, clashes of wit. He only hoped that Aristide would not unnecessarily antagonize this officer.

"Damned riffraff," came Josefina's angry voice. "Do you call them soldiers? Look at them!"

Hewitt wheeled Coco to where he could lean down and peer into the carriage. "One saucy word from you," he said between his teeth, "and you're the first thing I give up to them."

On came the soldiers, slowing to a walk as they approached the carriage. One of the riflemen unslung his weapon and carried it across his belly, at the ready. Now that they were closer, Hewitt could see that few of them wore anything resembling a uniform. The officer wore an ancient cap that surely had come down from the Army of Emperor Maximilian. The men wore faded blue, with wide, straw hats. Only the officer had boots; the enlisted men wore only thong *huaraches.*

Josefina glared back at Hewitt. "But when I see men like that pretending to be soldiers," she said, "I am ashamed to call myself a Mexican."

"You should be," Hewitt said. "It's people like you, taking all you can out of Mexico and doing nothing for her, who have impoverished this country to where it can't even clothe its soldiers. By God, someday the world will see what smart soldiers those fellows can be, but you won't. You'll be in Paris, complaining about the revolution and waiting for your money to run out."

Aristide chuckled softly. "There, *hija*, is the future, as I've so often told you. I'm glad I won't be here to see it, but it's coming."

Hewitt saw the girl turn her face away from the soldiers and glare angrily at nothing with that bitter look that robbed her of everything attractive. "Just keep quiet," he told her, "and I don't care how you feel."

He turned Coco again and walked him out to meet the soldiers. The stallion wanted to fight and was hard to handle. Hewitt deliberately managed him with one hand, keeping his left on his hip. Probably any of these soldiers was a better horseman than he, but let them see that he was master of the stallion! Those impressions counted.

As the soldiers neared him, he shifted Coco's reins to his left hand and raised his right, palm outward, in a gesture of peace. The stallion bugled a challenge at the sorry horses of the troops, and some of the army horses flinched back uneasily.

"*Buenas tardes, señor,*" he called.

"Hello," the officer replied. "You're American, are you not? I speak your language fine."

He halted his little squad no more than twenty feet away. He could have been anywhere from thirty to sixty, a lean, swarthy, sun-dried, seasoned man with a dark, heavy mustache. He had shaved this morning, and probably his shirt had been washed overnight. But he was not a barracks soldier, and he was far more at home in the saddle than he would have been in an office chair. On his shoulders he wore the pips of a captain.

"Yes, sir, Captain," Hewitt said. "I'm an old soldier myself."

"In the American Army?"

"Yes, sir. Headquarters Company, Presidio of San Francisco. But a long time ago, sir, a long time ago!"

He thought the officer relaxed a little, but not much. "What are you doing here?"

"I am escorting this Mexican family to the United States."

"Why do they need an American escort in Mexico?"

With his left hand, Hewitt indicated Nicolas and his men sitting their restless horses in formation behind the carriage. "I said escort, not guard, sir," he said. "They are under the protection of Mexicans, as you can see. My company represents this family in their business affairs in the United States, and I do them this courtesy. If I may offer my card, sir?"

With his left hand, he managed to fish one of his business cards out of his wallet. He held it out but made no move to bring it to the officer. He could only hope that Nicolas realized that the officer had already committed a serious tactical error by riding so close. He had lost the advantage his rifles gave him and was outgunned by the escort behind the carriage.

The officer murmured an order. The youth who carried the rifle across his belly rode forward and held out the gun. Hewitt slipped the card between the boy's fingers and the worn walnut of the throat of his rifle stock.

The young soldier whirled his horse, defiantly presenting his back, and returned to the line to offer the card to the officer. The captain studied it a long time. He could read English, clearly, but Bankers Bonding and Indemnity Company meant nothing to him.

"Cheyenne," he said, "that's somewhere in the mountains, ain't it?"

"In Wyoming, yes, sir."

"This is Señor Castañeda and his family, ain't it?"

"Yes, sir."

"What affairs do they have in Wyoming? I think you are lying to me, Mr. American Hewitt."

"I am not lying, sir," Hewitt replied, "and I don't like to be called a liar at gunpoint."

"No one is pointing a gun at you."

"No, but there are helpless women in the carriage, and I'm not a fool, sir. I know a threat when I see one."

"I am glad you understand," the officer said softly, letting the card fall from his hand to the ground. "We are going to take your horses, Mr. American Hewitt. I am taking possession of them in the name of my government, for the national patrimony. I hope you will not be so foolish as to resist."

Coco made a savage lunge forward. Hewitt hauled him back violently, making him squat. "Damn it, sir, behave!" he said to the horse.

He looked at the officer levelly. "I have no will in this matter, Captain," he said. "Señor Castañeda will not willingly yield the horses he needs to take the ladies of his family to safety. He has ordered his escort to fight rather than give up the horses. I have no choice, as you can see. I must fight at his side."

"Not on that horse, you won't," the captain said. "I will not risk injuring him. Please to dismount him."

Hewitt did not look back at Nicolas, but he raised his voice sharply: *"Nicolas! No cedemos nada, entiendes? Tenemos órdenes."*

We give up nothing, understand? We have our orders. He could only hope that Nicolas knew a good bluff when he heard one. *"Sí, señor,"* Nicolas said, and without looking back, Hewitt knew when the guard broke ranks and formed again between the carriage and the troops, behind him.

There was always one critical, make-or-break moment. You could not let yourself be bullied, but neither could you leave your adversary without a graceful way of making his own point.

"There is a better way, Captain," Hewitt said.

"No. On Mexican soil," the captain said, "there is no other way. You will obey the law."

Without understanding a word, Nicolas had sensed the showdown. Behind Hewitt, the ten guns of the mounted guard slid out of their holsters. They were all armed with .45 Colts, and they were all good shots. Aristide was proud of his guards, and had not stinted on ammunition for practice nor on money for prizes. They were simple, illiterate ranch hands. Their loyalty to Aristide was complete, and they were spoiling for a fight.

They did not like all this talk in English—and neither did the soldiers, who were tired, ill-armed compared to Aristide's men, and far from anxious to fight. Again Hewitt held up his hand, palm outward, warning Nicolas that he was still talking peace.

"You want horses, sir," Hewitt said, still respectfully but with a bite of impatience in his voice, "and we have women with us and cannot spare horses. But Señor Castañeda will be proud to pay money, and there are horses for sale elsewhere."

He let it hang there. The captain, after a taut moment, shook his head. "No! You cannot buy freedom from the law," he said. "First, your horses. Then we may talk about the money."

In the carriage, Josefina said, "Damn it, Hewitt, don't you beg!" Aristide muttered something in French. She replied in the same language, her voice rising angrily: "You have no honor, Father, if you will bargain with thieves. I would rather die."

Aristide chuckled and went on, still in French, "That is your taste, but you may not make such a decision for Helen and our unborn child."

"Shut her up," Hewitt snarled, "or, by God, I will let these soldiers silence her. I do not permit her to butt into my business."

"You will not permit?" Josefina cried. "*You* will not permit *me* to speak?"

The carriage door flew open and she came tumbling out, a slim figure in black and white, with a smart little French hat on her pile of black hair. Rage had brought a flush to her tawny cheeks and made her eyes sparkle. She took a step—another step—away from the carriage.

Hewitt slid out of the saddle, holding Coco's reins with his right hand. With his left, he removed his hat and made an extravagant bow.

"Captain," he said, "I beg to present Señorita Josefina, who has assumed command. Josefina, to hell with you. I'm heading for the border."

Not a sound came from the ragged line of ragged soldiers as they stared at her. Hewitt thought they were still more interested in horses than they were in the girl, but she had a perfect right to suspect that all those coldly angry, black eyes were mentally undressing her. She had courage, but not that much. She looked beseechingly at Hewitt, who did not condescend to look back at her.

"Into the carriage," he said, "or I surrender you to them on their own terms. If your father wishes to buy you back, that is his affair. But you will obey instantly or face the consequences."

"Please, Josefina," Helen said, from the carriage, "don't make things more difficult for your poor father. You promised you'd keep your temper."

You had to give someone like Josefina an easy retreat, too. The girl got back into the carriage.

"How much money?" the captain asked.

"One thousand American dollars," said Hewitt.

"It is not enough," the captain said, shaking his head. "He is a rich man, and the President's enemy. If he and his women have to walk barefoot to the border, begging their food, it is only justice."

Hewitt let him wait a moment for an answer. "One thousand dollars," he said, then. He repeated it in Spanish, slowly, for the benefit of the soldiers: "*Uno mil dolares Americanos, señor, uno mil dolares.*"

The captain heard the mutter of wonder from his own men, saw their eagerness, and sensed the complete collapse of their ardor to fight.

"That we see the money," he said in Spanish.

"The money, Aristide," Hewitt said in English. "Let the maid bring it to me."

In a moment, the carriage door opened again and Socorro got out, carrying a handful of paper currency. She put it in Hewitt's hand, and he held it up for the soldiers to see. Hewitt wished that it were gold coin, but these were border men. Enough of them had seen American currency to recognize it.

"Bring it here," the captain said.

"No," Hewitt said. "Send your man for it."

"I still give the orders," the captain said, his eyes narrowing.

Hewitt shook his head. The captain snapped an order in Spanish. The youth with the Mauser kicked his horse forward. He cuddled the cumbersome rifle against him with his arm while he reached for the money. Hewitt put it into the boy's hand and then, warned by some inner tingle of dread, stepped back quickly.

The youth brandished the money in his fist, over his head. "Now the girl, too, and the horses," he shouted in Spanish.

Hewitt dropped to his knees on the ground as Nicolas fired. He heard the bullet screech over his head and thud into the young soldier's body. Another shot crashed, and toppled boy, rifle, and all from the saddle. The handful of currency floated to the ground.

CHAPTER FIVE

Hewitt fired at the captain's horse. He knew he had had more than his share of luck when he saw the slug strike between the horse's eyes. It dropped inertly. Coco went up on his hind legs. Hewitt got the reins twisted around his left hand and went up with him.

He got his feet under him and dug in his heels. He shouted in Spanish, "No more shooting, no more shooting! I will kill the first man to fire his gun."

The captain was trapped with one foot under his dead horse. Coco gave up fighting. "Help him, man," Hewitt snarled at one of the soldiers, in Spanish.

The man dismounted, took hold of the captain's saddle horn, and lifted. Hewitt gestured with his .45, and another soldier got down and helped. The captain pulled his foot out from under the dead horse and stood up, testing the leg painfully. Hewitt could not help but admire the way he kept his dignity. It hurt to stand, but he stood.

The horse of the dead rifleman had run a few yards and then stopped. He stood with his head down, gaunt, tired, hungry. Hewitt ordered one of the soldiers to catch him and bring him back.

Shifting back to English, he said, "Your man started it, sir."

"You have fired against the President's troops," the captain replied. "You are outlaws, all of you."

"Very well," said Hewitt, "we're outlaws. I want your rifles. It's no disgrace to hand them over at gunpoint, sir. You will please give the order."

The captain snapped an order in Spanish. The other two riflemen kicked their horses forward and, at a nod from Hewitt, dropped their weapons beside that of the dead man.

"Now," said Hewitt, "have someone pick up the money."

"No man of mine," said the officer, "will touch that money. You killed one of my men. You may not buy back a soldier's blood with money."

"Your man was a damned fool," Hewitt said. "We are not to blame for his folly."

The captain said nothing. His men stared greedily at the currency on the ground. The carriage creaked as Aristide stepped out of it. Frowning, he studied the captain's face.

"Martínez," he said in English. "That's your name, Gilberto Martínez, the son of Raul Martínez. Your father and I were cadets together, before he went into the Foreign Office. New Orleans—he became consul in New Orleans, did he not?"

The captain ignored him completely, exuding hatred and contempt. "Get back inside," Hewitt said, "and let's get moving, Aristide. We have lost enough time."

Aristide got back into the carriage. Hewitt gave an order to the coachman, who spoke to the two harness teams. The four horses had rested long enough. They started willingly and hit their fine, fast walk.

Nicolas and his men formed up again, but they did not follow the carriage. They holstered their guns and sat impassively, awaiting orders. Knowing that they had him covered, Hewitt picked up the money, straightened it into a neat pack, and folded it into his pocket.

"Don't try to follow us, Captain Martínez," he said.

"You have fired on the President's soldiers," Martínez replied. "You are outlaws. My turn will come."

"You had better have your men under better control before you call them soldiers, and don't speak of outlaws when your own man accepts Señor Castañeda's money and then proposes to steal his daughter."

Martínez did not reply. He mounted the horse his dead rifleman had ridden and made a motion with his hand for his men to fall in behind him.

"These are bad times, Captain," Hewitt said, "but you only make them worse. I'm sorry this happened, but your man started it. Be damn sure of one thing, we will defend ourselves against anyone who threatens Mexican women!"

He had to muscle Coco unmercifully to get him to stand while he mounted, but it suited him that the troops should see that he could handle the horse. He raised his hand in a salute, which Martínez ignored, and set out after the carriage at a gallop.

He did not have to give Nicolas orders. Nicolas held his men until Hewitt had reached the carriage. Then he sent them, one at a time, after Hewitt. He brought up the rear himself, making it clear to the soldiers that if they would make further trouble it would be at their peril. The three who had picked up the Mausers stowed them, regretfully, in the baggage boot behind the carriage, at Hewitt's orders.

No one inside the carriage was saying a word as Hewitt reached it, and he did not look at them. Only a few minutes had passed when Aristide gave a sharp cry.

"Stop! My wife is ill. *Alto, cochero, alto!*"

The coachman halted the teams so abruptly that the leaders went up on their hind legs. Hewitt had to spur Coco around the carriage in order to dismount and open the door. A backward glance showed him that Captain Martínez and his troops had started to move back toward the cart, but had halted to watch the carriage. Nicolas immediately formed up his men in a protective line a hundred yards to the rear.

Helen stumbled out into Hewitt's arms, with Aristide behind her. Between them, they held her while she vomited violently. Aristide looked at Hewitt with terror in his eyes. Hewitt shook his head reassuringly.

"Take it easy, ma'am," he said. "Everything's going to be all right."

"He was just an ignorant boy," she moaned between retchings, "and now he's dead. I saw him shot down, killed. My God, why?"

The maid, Socorro, got out of the carriage and enfolded the woman in her arms, crooning to her as she would have to a baby. In the carriage, Josefina watched with both pity and impatience on her face.

"*Gracias, gracias, ya estoy bien,*" Helen said to the maid. But she continued to lean on the old woman for support, and her face was pallid. In the distance, the troops remained motionless. Captain Martínez took off his hat to shade his eyes as he watched.

"But, Helen," said Josefina, "he brought it on himself. That's why we're leaving Mexico. This damned Díaz and his thugs—"

Hewitt turned on her in fury. "Shut up! You have done nothing but cause trouble since we started. What she needs is help—kindness—not one of your damned lectures."

She glared back rebelliously, but when Socorro and

Aristide helped Helen back into the carriage, Josefina was the one who placed the cushions so that Helen could lie back in greater comfort. It was Josefina who opened a little case of cosmetics and took out a bottle of cologne and began wetting Helen's wrists and temples with it.

The lilac scent of the cologne filled the carriage with a haunting suggestion of another life, of better times that might be gone forever. Hewitt closed the door of the carriage and swung up into the saddle. When he looked back, Martínez and his little squad had already gotten in motion toward the sea to the west. The lad who drove the cart was turning it to follow them.

It was doubtful that they would find anything. Horses, forage, and food were scarce. Anyone who owned anything had long since secreted it. Horses would be hidden in out-of-the-way canyons, guarded by small boys who would not be missed. Hay would be stacked in small, brush-covered ricks, and grain and food for humans would be buried. Those American dollars could have coaxed some of it out of hiding, but probably not enough to make the sacrifice of pride worthwhile.

The coachman put the teams in motion. The carriage rocked on. In a moment, Helen sat up and began talking in a normal tone of voice. Nicolas closed up behind them. He and his men searched the terrain continuously with their eyes, made nervous and edgy by the brush with the troops. The next such confrontation would find them quicker to fire and harder to restrain.

It seemed to Hewitt that the heat had increased, despite the stronger breeze coming off the Gulf. The thick haze made it impossible to see the horizon, but Hewitt was sure that black storm clouds were piling up all around them. It could rain like the end of the world here, and it was one more peril he had to take into consideration. Once the rain came, they dared not be caught near any of the dry channels that carried storm waters.

On the other hand, a good rain would bring at least temporary relief from the heat and humidity, but Hewitt doubted that rain would come. Every day had been like this, and every night. Except for the early-morning hours, the air remained at the saturation point, so sweating gave no relief to man or beast. The sweat did not evaporate and take the body heat with it. It simply dripped off, drying out the tissues without giving relief.

The women dozed and Aristide sat staring at nothing. Late in the afternoon, Hewitt heard the women talking and caught a signal from Aristide that they wanted to make a comfort stop. Hewitt had the coachman pull into the first shade and swing his horses around so that they caught the sluggish breeze in their faces. The women got out of the carriage and vanished into the thicket of brush. Nicolas and his men spread out to cover the carriage from all directions.

A good man, this young Nicolas, Hewitt thought. He was as smart and decisive as he was devoted and brave. It would be too bad for Mexico if she lost many like him.

Hewitt dismounted and walked to the side of the carriage. "How do you feel, Aristide?" he asked. "You're not standing the heat very well, are you?"

"It is not the heat, Jeff," Aristide replied. "It is sad to think of Gilberto. He's a good man, with a good education, yet what future can he have here?"

"That's his choice to make. I'm not sure he's wrong, not by any means."

Aristide sighed. "Oh yes, Gilberto's a patriot, but then it's easy for him. He has nothing to lose."

"How so?"

"His father opposed Juárez. He lost everything. That's

what is so cruel about this Díaz regime. Don Porfirio will let young men like Gilberto sacrifice themselves—their souls, their futures, their lives—and for what?"

"Perhaps," said Hewitt, "for Mexico. You said it yourself—he's a patriot. There are times in every nation's history when all patriots look like fools, I suppose. The leaders of the American Revolution looked like fools once."

Aristide frowned at him. "Are you deserting me, friend Hewitt?"

Hewitt shook his head. "This is a business deal with me. Conrad got me into it. He wants you delivered COD in Texas—very well, that's what I'll do. Unless," he added thoughtfully, "your daughter makes it impossible."

"Poor Josefina," said Aristide. "One foot in the world of Mexico, the other in New York, London, Paris—she isn't sure where. She needs a strong hand, and unfortunately I have not been a domineering father."

"She needs," said Hewitt, "to be spanked."

"Agreed."

Hewitt started to mount his horse again. Aristide made a motion to stop him.

"Jeff," he said, "Conrad is very fond of you. I suppose you know that."

"I'm very fond of him. He's a good partner and a better friend."

"He says you would be better off married. He says you are not by nature a lone wolf. You need a wife, a home, and children, and until you get them, you will drift from woman to woman until you become cynical and unhappy. I presume that an arranged marriage would be a shocking idea to you, at least at first."

"At first," said Hewitt, "and at last, too. I'm not a marrying man and I don't see why we need discuss it."

"My wife," said Aristide, "suggests that you're the man to make Josefina happy, and she's never wrong about these things—never! I would be happy to discuss it with you seriously, when we reach safety across the river."

"We have already discussed it, just now," Hewitt said. "Thank you, Aristide, but it's impossible."

They could hear the women talking as they returned to the carriage. Aristide dropped his voice. "Will you let my wife talk to you about it?"

"It would be a waste of time."

Hewitt mounted, and let Aristide get out and help the women back into the carriage. Aristide's wife seemed to have recovered from the nervous convulsion caused by the shooting of the young soldier, and Josefina was somewhat subdued, as though she had finally realized that she could not arrogantly storm her way through this little segment of her life. In repose, her face was almost beautiful.

The carriage doors closed. Hewitt waved a signal to Nicolas. The coachman swung his teams around into the twin wheelmarks of the road.

Nearly two hours later, Nicolas spurred up to ride beside Hewitt. He pointed ahead. "Charco Verdugo," he said.

Since Nicolas understood no English, Hewitt had to speak in Spanish. "Your eyes are better than mine. How far?"

"Three miles, more or less."

"Something worries you, Nico. What?"

"The horses."

"What about the horses?"

"Where are they? There are many horses, and not much grass. The wind has fallen, yet we see no dust. I have driven horses here before, on such a day as this. The dust rises a mile—two miles!—into the sky."

"What do you think I should do, Nico?"

"Let me send a man on ahead. One with a good head and a good horse, that if there is trouble, he can get back to tell us. I am much worried."

"As you think best, Nico."

With a sharp call, the young commander summoned a man and snapped terse orders to him. He had the man take one of the Mausers with him.

"If there is trouble," he said, "do not become a part of it, but return at once. If it is possible, signal us with two shots of the rifle. I tell you, man, take care! I don't like the look of things."

The man was almost twice Nicolas's age, but he took the youth's orders without objection and his advice seriously. He put his powerful horse into an easy canter, and soon was gone from sight in the heavy heat-haze that shimmered over the road ahead.

It seemed to Hewitt that it was only minutes later when they heard the heavy *thud thud* of the rifle, two shots let off as close together as the man could fire them. Hewitt told Nicolas to pull his men closer around the carriage and keep a sharp eye out in all directions.

Coco wanted a run, the heat notwithstanding. Aristide called out something as Hewitt passed the carriage, but Hewitt ignored him. In a few moments, he could make out the vague, dark blots in the sky that were the five cottonwoods around Charco Verdugo. He passed a pair of Aristide's horses, and then three or four more.

Still more horses appeared, pulling at the short, wiry, dry grass that grew so sparsely here, but it was clear that the big herd was scattered. Most of them were probably long gone.

Nico's man did not appear until Hewitt rode down into the shallow depression in which lay the spring-fed pond

that gave this place its name. The pond had been tram-
pled by the herd until its banks were churned into acres
of mud, but the water itself had settled and now looked
clear again. Every horse had been able to drink, that was
certain.

Nico's man pointed silently to where a human body
dangled on a rope that was suspended from a horizontal
limb of one of the tall cottonwoods. The wrists had been
tied behind and a horse whipped out from under, and the
man had died hard, strangled instead of dying mercifully
with a broken neck.

"*Los soldados,*" Nico's man said, pointing to the tracks
of shod horses around the dangling body.

The clothing looked familiar, but the face was so con-
torted and blue, and the dry tongue protruded so far between the fly-covered lips, that it was hard for Hewitt to
recognize the dead man. But there could be no mistake.
This was John Singleton Mosby Kirk, the kid he had put
in charge of the guardia gringo and the horse herd.

Hewitt held the horse still while Nico's man swarmed
up and stood on his saddle to cut down the body. Together, then, they followed the tracks until they could
have a pretty good idea of what had happened. Everywhere the tracks of shod horses were plain over those of
Aristide's herd. Once the soldiers had rounded up a sub-
stantial part of the herd, they had turned them north by
west and pushed them hard.

"To Reynosa?" said Hewitt, in Spanish.

"*Sin duda,*" Nico's man replied. Without doubt.

Of George Boney, Orval Honeycutt, Dugan Peeke, and
Blackie Randall there was no sign.

CHAPTER SIX

They had no shovel, not even a spoon with which to dig a grave for Mose Kirk. With a sharp stick and a flat, edged rock, they hacked away furiously at the ground under one of the cottonwoods. When they got down to damp soil, it went faster.

When the grave was three feet deep, Hewitt sent the Mexican to gather rocks to put on the grave. He undressed the body enough to examine it. There were no bullet holes, but there was evidence that Mose had been beaten over the head with something. A gun barrel or trigger guard might have made those marks. Mose had not bled much, and chances were that he had never been knocked out.

But he would have been at least dazed, and in a lot of pain. He had made *somebody* mad enough to want to hammer him with a gun, probably after his wrists had been tied behind him. The wrists were tied not with the untanned buckskin so common here in Mexico, but with strong, tanned leather of a good grade. A calf-tie or pig-gin' string, Hewitt thought. Working cowhands carried them at branding time, to pull a calf's feet together while he was being branded.

A man got used to using his own piggin' strings. You

could buy them from any harness shop or saddler. They were made from scrap, from strips of strong, flexible back-leather too narrow for any other use. But good ones—piggin' strings like this one—could cost you fifteen cents apiece.

Hewitt put the strong leather tie in his pocket. With luck, he might someday identify the man who owned it. It might or might not identify a murderer. If the troops had hanged Mose, they could have tied his wrists behind his back with a piggin' string taken forcibly from some other captive—George Boney, Dugan Peeke, Blackie Randall, or Orval Honeycutt, for instance.

On the other hand—

They had the grave well covered with rocks by the time the carriage arrived, and they could help hold the two harness teams while they were unhitched. The horses were all crazy to get to the water. Aristide and Socorro both got out and helped hold them. Had they been permitted, they would quickly have drunk themselves to death.

It was almost dark, and as hot as ever, when the carriage teams could at last be tied to trees and fed a little barley from the luggage boot on the carriage. The vicious jijenes had been left behind, but now a cloud of voracious mosquitoes arose over the ponds. There could be no less attractive place to camp, but they had no choice.

Nicolas's men gathered brush for cooking fires and mosquito smudges. Socorro got out the big iron pot of chili stew and the leg of veal, which was all the food they had left from the ranch. She put on a can to heat water for the tea that Aristide demanded with every meal.

Josefina made Helen get out of the carriage while she prepared a bed for her. The girl, Hewitt thought, was probably not as contrite as she acted, but she at least had the good sense to know that she had lost this battle of wills. No one could have been kinder or more helpful than Josefina was to her young stepmother.

Nicolas put out pickets, ordering them to stay afoot, lead their horses, and patrol ceaselessly. Thunder was rumbling far to the west when Socorro at last called them to supper. She would have fed Aristide and his family first, but Aristide would have none of this.

"We are a retreating army," he said, "and the fighting men eat first."

Nicolas and his men came in pairs to take their food and slip away, either to sleep or to go on picket duty. To Hewitt, it was ironic that they were fed in fine English china, with handwrought, antique silver spoons. He declined to eat until the ten-man guard had been fed.

He then sat down on the ground with the family, near the cooking fire, with a mosquito smudge-fire going upwind. The stew was so *picante* with the fiery peppers that Hewitt grinned at the thought of what Conrad Meuse would have said. He detested spicy food, even some Viennese cooking. "Only a savage would eat that stuff," he had told Hewitt once, when he caught him over a bowl of chili con carne in a Cheyenne trail-drivers' restaurant.

The horses, their curiosity aroused by the fire, came wandering in to drink at the charco again. "How many do you think there are left?" Aristide asked.

"About half," Hewitt replied. "Or, say forty or fifty. They got away with most of them."

"Perhaps my men will return and help round them up."

"Could be," Hewitt said with a grunt.

"I do not blame young Kirk," Aristide went on thoughtfully, "but I really do feel it was the wrong time to make the change."

Hewitt, thinking of Kirk in his grave, with his swollen

tongue protruding from his dehydrated mouth, did not reply. One of the Mexican guards brought in another armload of brush and laid some of the greenest on the smudge-fire, to raise more smoke to keep away the mosquitoes.

Aristide cocked his ear. "We'll surely get a good wetting tonight."

"Before very long, too, from the sound of it," said Hewitt.

"You must come into the carriage with us if it does rain."

"No, I have a waterproof sheet and a blanket. That's all I need."

"Really, Jeff, I can't allow you to stay out in the rain."

Hewitt said irritably, "Nicolas and his men will be out in it. The trees are the only shelter for miles. If there are troops on the move, they'll head for here. I want to be available if I'm needed."

Lightning began to play in the west and south. Helen murmured something about how lightning always made her uneasy. Josefina jumped up and offered her stepmother her hand.

"Come, let's get into the carriage and pull up the windows," she said. "We can let down the shades if the lightning frightens you."

"Really, I'm all right. You're not to worry about me, any of you, do you hear?"

Another sheet of lightning flared across the whole northwest quadrant of the sky. Helen snatched at Josefina's hand and started to get up. She fell back down again as Josefina put her hands to her cheeks and began screaming one hoarse scream after another.

Hewitt got to her and caught her by both arms. Another flash of lightning, closer still, lighted up the whole charco. The girl jerked an arm loose and pointed to the rope that still dangled from the limb where Mose Kirk had kicked himself to death.

"He's dead, he's dead, it was Mose hanged there, wasn't it?" Josefina shrieked. "They killed him, they hanged him, where is he, what did you do with him?"

Not until the rain began did she get control of herself, and then she would not go into the carriage until she had gotten the truth from Hewitt. Aristide quickly got Helen away and into the carriage, and just as quickly came back to hear what Hewitt had to say:

"There's no question about it, there were troops here— well-trained regulars, with shod horses, probably one of the crack regiments at Reynosa, since that's where they went with the horses."

"And they—those murderers—those ghouls—they hanged Kirk?" Aristide said. "They hanged that mere boy?"

"He was no mere boy," Hewitt said, "and I'm not convinced that they hanged him. Where are George Boney and the others? We sure as hell didn't find their bodies."

"You surely don't suspect them of betraying me and hanging Kirk!"

"I don't know what happened, Aristide—whether they turned traitor or merely ran for it. One thing is sure, Kirk stayed and tried to fight it out. That's more than they did."

"But *you* sent him here to die," Josefina said, between chattering teeth. "Where did you bury him? I want to see him. I have the *right* to see him!"

"But, *hija,* it is nothing to you," Aristide said. "It is too bad, yes. I feel great sorrow inside myself, too. But how will it help for you to see his body?"

Hewitt caught his eye and shook his head angrily. What had begun as a few spattering drops had become a steady drizzle, and by the sound of it, worse was still to come.

"Both of you get into the carriage," Hewitt said. "Josefina, go with your father. That's an order. I don't want a screaming girl on my hands if the soldiers return."

She stumbled as Aristide led her away through the rain and darkness. Hewitt heard the door of the carriage slam. In a moment he went to the luggage boot, opened it, and groped around until he found his bedroll. He had no waterproof slicker—but then neither did Nicolas and his men. He got out the bedroll, wrapped in the waterproof sheet, and threw it under the carriage, where it would remain reasonably dry until he needed it.

The rain came pounding down harder and harder. The fires had long since gone out. The lightning diminished and then stopped altogether, but the downpour kept on for almost an hour before it slackened slightly.

He heard Nicolas's voice, and responded. The lad stood near where the campfires had burned, holding his horse. None of his men could sleep in the rain, he reported, so all were out patrolling. He had, he said, thought things over and come to the conclusion that the soldiers would not return tonight, and probably not tomorrow. They would have all they could do to handle the horses they had rounded up and get them to Reynosa in the storm.

Nicolas felt strongly that Hewitt should sleep while he had the chance. A little uneasily, Hewitt agreed. He took his bedroll from under the carriage and carried it to the dubious shelter of one of the cottonwoods. There was mud everywhere, but the storm had moved on and the rain was almost over.

He folded his waterproof so he would have half of it under him, half over him, and used his folded blanket for a mattress. As the rain died, the mosquitoes came out. He pulled the waterproof over his head and closed his eyes.

CHAPTER SEVEN

It was broad daylight when Nico came stealing through the mud to awaken him. Nicolas jerked a thumb toward the spot where they had had their cooking fire last night.

Two of his men had killed a calf and were dressing it. Another had a small fire going at last, and was feeding it tenderly with wet wood, a shred at a time. Others had encircled the band of horses that had come down to the charco to drink. Hewitt counted twenty-four of them—all the best of the herd, the strongest, wildest, and most-spirited, which had refused to be driven.

Beside the fire, two men squatted. They looked at him apprehensively as he and Nicolas came toward them. George Boney and Orval Honeycutt were drawn and haggard. They had been soaked to the skin and still were not dry, and there was no sign of their horses.

"Where are Peeke and Randall?" Hewitt asked.

It was Boney who answered. "They played out. They's back yander four, five miles. I said we'd fetch them horses and grub. How long's it goin' to take to fry up some of this goddamn meat? It's takin' him forever, and where the hell is that maid to cook it?"

"For somebody that hasn't done anything right for two

days," Hewitt said, "you've got a pretty big mouth, haven't you, Boney?"

Boney came stiffly to his feet. "You got a mighty big mouth yourself," he said, "but you take that gun off, and we'll see."

"You had a gun yesterday. What happened to it?"

"Them sojers took it. They—"

"What happened to Mose Kirk?"

"They strung him up, and it served him right. He like to got all of us killed. Take that gun off before you try to rawhide me. Make it man-to-man."

"I'm not going to fight you, Boney. I'd chop you to mincemeat."

"God damn you, Hewitt—" Boney choked.

He charged, fists pumping. He was, Hewitt estimated, close to fifty. He had been a tough man in his day, but never as tough as he thought he was. Now he was all in from having walked all night in the rain, but too crazed with rage to have good sense.

Hewitt met his charge head-on, without trying to side-step. He had to give way to sheer weight, taking three backward steps and covering up to take Boney's big fists on his shoulders and arms. He saw his chance and snapped a sharp left jab into Boney's belly, low down.

He doubled Boney up and could have put him down with a right cross to the jaw. Instead, he got behind him, took him by both shoulders, and sent him spinning. Boney went down hard, sat up slowly, and looked up at Hewitt. He was as full of rage as ever, but animal instinct warned him not to try it again.

"You're in no shape to fight me," Hewitt said. "I want to know what happened yesterday."

"You give me somethin' to eat and one hour of rest," Boney said, "just one hour, and we'll try that again."

"You never will be in shape to fight me," said Hewitt. "I want to know what happened. Are you going to tell me or am I going to have to kick it out of you?"

The fire was blazing merrily now, and one of the Mexican guards was slicing thin cutlets from the carcass of the calf. Nicolas brought some second-growth cottonwood switches with sharpened ends. At a nod from Hewitt, he handed one to Boney and one to Honeycutt. The two men impaled several slices of meat on them and held them over the fire to cook.

As they ate, they talked. Boney did most of the talking, and Hewitt had the impression that most of what he said was true. Boney was the kind who could look you in the eye and lie, but Honeycutt lacked that kind of guts. No doubt Boney had rehearsed him on the story during the long, long night's walk, but the dull-witted Honeycutt still had no confidence in his ability to make a lie stick.

The horses, Boney said, had been impossible to hold once they scented water. They ran the last five or six miles as hard as they could go, and plunged into the waterhole so fast that they piled on top of one another. Only their sheer number had kept them from drinking themselves to death. They fought over the water for an hour before they gave up and began looking for grass.

"A goddamn horse," said Boney, "ain't got a lick of sense. He'll founder himself if you let him. Now you take a mule, he knows better. A mule will—"

"I know about mules," Hewitt said. "When did the troops show up?"

"About the time the herd got its bellies full. Wasn't nothin' left then but mud."

The troops had come at the trot, in two columns of twos—a full regiment, apparently, and a good one, since their uniforms were almost new. Only the seasoned and disciplined regulars got uniforms from Uncle Porfirio.

"This here Colonel Domínguez, he talked American as good as you or me," said Boney. "He asked us who—"

"Wait a minute," Hewitt said. "Mose Kirk hadn't got here yet?"

"No. This here colonel, he wanted to know who owned these horses. Like you told me to do, I said we was deliverin' them to the remount officer in Matamoros. He said there wasn't no remount officer in Matamoros. I said I didn't know nothing about that. I said I was supposed to let some Mexican general in Matamoros have them."

"Where were the horses all this time?"

"Why, feedin' around here, close."

"And the regiment came in two columns all the way? They didn't fan out to take charge of the herd?"

"I just done told you, Mr. Hewitt, they come straight in like they was on parade. Why?"

"I'm only wondering why the hell you stood there like knots on a log and left the horses bunched. Why didn't you scatter them? There were four of you. You had four of the best and fastest horses in Mexico. You could have scattered that herd to hell and gone and been out of rifle range before they knew what was happening."

"Mr. Hewitt, they was nearly seven hundred of 'em. Four against seven hundred—why—"

"They approached you politely, didn't they?"

"Yes, they sure did, but—"

"For all they knew, Uncle Porfirio himself owned these horses. You had all the advantage, man. You could have scattered them and rejoined us. Instead, you made them a present of half the herd! When did Mose Kirk get here?"

A shadow crossed Boney's face and his eyes fell. "We's arguin'," he said, "this colonel and me. He's tellin' me we's goin' to deliver these horses to Reynosa, and he'll give us a receipt for them same as 'they would in Matamoros. The sojers would help deliver them. In fact, he'd give me a receipt right then and there!"

Boney reached for more meat. Hewitt waited for him to go on. When he did not, Hewitt said, "What really happened is that you *took* his receipt, didn't you?"

"What else could I do, Mr. Hewitt? He didn't ask me, he *told* me. Well then, one of the sojers said something in Mexican, and the colonel seen this fool kid of a Mose Kirk comin'.'"

Mose had ridden in boldly and presented the letter relieving Boney of command. The colonel had demanded to see it, and Boney had handed it over. The colonel had smiled and handed it back.

"Too bad!" he said. "Young man, I have already taken charge of the herd in the name of the Mexican government. I'm going to have to take you and your men along, too. You'll be released as soon as I have delivered the horses to my general in Reynosa."

"Like hell I will," Mose shouted, snatching off his hat.

He whirled his horse and raced him through the bunched horses that had started to wander back to the charco. A couple of troopers snatched out carbines to fire at him, but the colonel told them not to take a chance of hitting a valuable horse.

One thing was sure, this Colonel Domínguez was a quick thinker. What happened to Kirk was not really important, so long as they got the horses. The colonel snapped an order that sent his men out at the gallop to round up the herd. They had been on the march all day, and their horses were no match for the Castañeda horses. Sheer numbers made it possible for them to bunch fifty-six horses quickly, and hold them tightly, beside the charco.

Kirk had ridden on out of sight. The moment the soldiers put the herd in motion, Kirk came racing in again, firing his gun in the air. The astonished soldiers had all they could do to hold the herd together.

Straight into the herd Kirk rode, screaming at the top of his voice. To Boney, he looked crazy. He did not even seem to see the more than seven hundred soldiers that had formed a ring around the horses.

"He might as well of rode straight inter a brick wall," Boney said. "I seen one of them sojers jump onto Mose's horse and beat him over the haid with the butt of his gun. I jist cain't unnerstand how you'd put somebody like that in charge of anything, Mr. Hewitt. He purely didn't have good sense."

Which was surely the truest thing Boney had said so far, Hewitt reflected. Poor Kirk had thought himself invincible. He truly had been mad, and Josefina had made him that way. Even after they had muscled him down flat on his back on the ground, he had shouted threats at them.

Colonel Domínguez had to try three or four times to make the kid listen to him.

"You say that Aristide Castañeda owns these horses? Who is he, young man? I don't know him. It's not important, anyway. I have requisitioned these horses for the Mexican government."

"You cain't. Don Aristide won't stand fer it."

"I already have, and I'm rapidly losing patience with you. Are you going to help move these horses, or—"

"You son of a bitch, don't you expect me to help your goddamned thievin' government steal these horses."

The colonel's face flushed. His eyes snapped. He jerked his thumb at the horizontal limb that jutted out from the nearest cottonwood no more than fifteen feet above the ground.

One trooper tied two ropes together and thew them over the limb. He swarmed up them hand over hand, and made the end of one fast to the limb. He dropped the other—they had to be frugal about everything, these troopers—and slid to the ground.

They did not bother to make a hangman's noose with a big knot that would have a chance of snapping Kirk's head to one side sharply enough to break his neck. They simply slipped a noose over his head, set him on his own horse *behind* the saddle with his hands tied behind him, and gave the horse a sharp dig in the flanks with a thumb.

Boney doubted that Kirk understood what was happening to him until the last minute. He was still cursing the colonel, still vowing vengeance, when the horse jumped into a run and left him swinging back and forth, back and forth, under the cottonwood tree.

It took him a long time to die, it seemed to Boney. Hewitt saw Honeycutt shudder, and knew that the hanging had affected him still more. Neither they nor Dugan Peeke nor Blackie Randall were in any mood to argue when the colonel gave them orders to help haze the horse herd toward Reynosa.

One company had ridden with them; the other had remained to round up more horses. They gave it up quickly, however, and had only nine more head when they caught up with the herd only a few miles from the charco.

"So they got away with sixty-five altogether," Hewitt said. "The fifty-six they started with, plus the nine they brought up later."

"No, about forty-eight or fifty," Boney said. "They lost a few. Them damn army horses couldn't keep up with veal calves. So fin'ly they taken our horses and told us to start walkin', an' we did. I doubt if they reached the river with more than thirty or forty, because me and Orval seen several head back to'rds the waterhole."

"All right," Hewitt said, "catch what rest you can, because it's going to be a long walk to the river for you. Unless you can ride bareback."

"The river? I promised Dugan and Blackie—"

"We'll catch up to them. We're going to follow the herd, just as soon as we can get this herd together and put them on the trail."

"Christ, Hewitt, you must be loco! I told you, they's seven hundred of them sojers."

"Then you'll need all the rest you can get, won't you?"

There was no sign of life yet from the carriage. Hewitt walked away and left Boney staring at him, and knocked sharply on the carriage door. "We've got to hit the trail quickly, Aristide," he said when he heard the don's sleepy grumble inside. "Everybody up now, on the double!"

CHAPTER EIGHT

Hewitt let the procession go on ahead while he sat studying the cottonwood grove for a long time. He had seldom been so shaken by the death of a casual acquaintance as he had by Mose Kirk's. There was a tangle of conflicting loyalties, and perhaps a little treachery, and certainly a lot of selfishness, in the events leading up to that brutal hanging. He thought he understood most of them, and he could not help reproaching himself for not having understood them earlier, in time to keep the kid alive.

He took from his saddlebag the rope with which Mose had been hanged. He had told Nicolas to send a couple of his men back to retrieve it without calling attention to themselves, and to hand it over to him surreptitiously. It was clearly a Mexican rope, of braided leather, supple and strong. It would not have been sacrificed thus, had it been full length. This was what was left after some accident.

Hangman's Springs. He wished now that he had had Nico cut off that tempting horizontal limb entirely. No telling how many men had been hanged from it. No telling how many still would be.

He turned a rested—and restless—Coco and galloped him after the carriage. Boney and Honeycutt now rode on top of it, armed with captured Mausers as well as their own six-guns. One of Nicolas's men rode in attendance behind the carriage. The others, including Nico himself, had gone ahead with the horse herd.

They had managed to round up forty-one horses as they came in to drink this morning. Three more had joined the herd soon after leaving Charco Verdugo. Horses were gregarious creatures. Sometimes—today, for instance—it made them easier to manage.

The sun had come out and there was not a cloud in the sky, but it had unexpectedly turned cooler. There was a dry breeze from the northwest. If it held, they would make good time today.

He ignored Boney and Honeycutt as he pulled up beside the carriage. Aristide beamed at him. "Well, friend Hewitt," he said, "make us a prediction. When will we reach the river, and once we get there, can we cross it?"

"With luck," Hewitt said, "we could get there today. If I knew where to hit it, I could come closer to guessing whether we'll make it across with the carriage."

"You will think of something," Helen said, smiling. The night's sleep, even in the heat of the closed carriage, had restored her. The bright, coolish morning had contributed even more.

"I know I'll think of something, ma'am," he said, "but whether it'll work—that's the question."

"Mr. Meuse says you have never failed yet."

He made a face. "I think Conrad must have been giving you Sales Speech Sixteen B. That's not the way I hear it when we tot things up."

He glanced at Josefina, who looked sluggish, dull, and hopeless.

"*Como estás, señorita?*" he said gently.

Her eyes came up to meet his. *"Bien, gracias,"* she replied, as with an effort.

Her eyes dropped, and she stared at nothing.

"I remember walkin' along here," Honeycutt said. "Blackie and Dugan's still up ahaid som'ers."

"We'll find them if they're still alive," Hewitt replied.

"If they're still alive?" Boney said quickly, in alarm.

"Yes. The way you four handled things yesterday, I wouldn't be surprised to find they had been attacked by an enraged jackrabbit."

The two did not reply. They were following the trail of the horse herd expropriated by the troops. Even last night's hard rain had failed to wipe out the tracks. The herd was making a beeline for Reynosa, which, Hewitt estimated, was fifteen to twenty miles away.

He had no intention of following the trail much farther. Shortly they would find that Nicolas had left the northwesterly trail to head straight north. He himself did not know the river well, but one of his older men claimed to know of a place where they might, with luck, get over. They might have to abandon the carriage, but they could at least make it over to American territory with the women and, he hoped, their luggage and the horses.

The north side of the river was patrolled regularly by United States cavalry. It was not likely that Mexican troops would pursue them across the river, but Hewitt was far from sure of their reception by American troops. The United States was supporting the government of Porfirio Díaz, turning back rebels and bandits. It was not likely that they would surrender the women to the porfiristas, but the valuable horses were another proposition.

And so, Hewitt thought, might Aristide be. If Díaz made a point of it, and could get information to his consuls in Texas in time, Aristide could find himself in trouble. There would be no long, drawn-out extradition process, not on this border. He would be taken almost to the center of an international bridge by some unidentified local peace officers.

There, four or five of them would seize him and start running with him. They would let go just before they reached the dividing line. Aristide's momentum would carry him on across, so that he reentered Mexico without a hand on him. "Returned," the American peace officers' report would say, "of his own volition." The Mexicans called it *repatriacion corriendo*, "running repatriation."

"Once we're across—assuming, of course, that we're going to get across—where do you go then?" Hewitt asked.

"I have a little place in Corpus Christi," said Aristide. "Not much, but adequate, and it's on the railroad and telegraph line. I will decide what to do after I have received certain information."

"Two hundred miles beyond the river."

"Almost that," Aristide said serenely, "but we can proceed at our leisure, and we can buy harnesses—perhaps a buggy or two—tents—whatever we need. We will make a gay picnic procession of it."

I'll just bet you do, Hewitt thought, looking at the lifeless face of the girl. She was still numb from the shock of Kirk's death. One of these days, the reaction would come. If he knew her, it would be violent.

"I'm not sure I can attend your picnic all the way," he said. "I have to check on some affairs of my own."

"Oh, but it would be spoiled without you," Aristide cried. "You engaged to take us to safety, and I won't feel safe until I'm in my own house in Corpus Christi."

A gunshot rapped through the still air somewhere

ahead of them, and then another. On top of the carriage, Boney and Honeycutt sat up and gripped their heavy rifles harder. A look of alarm crossed Aristide's face.

"Take it easy," Hewitt said. "Nothing to worry about."

He gave Coco his head, and the big stud put his belly down and his nose out and ran the way a powerful horse, bred to run, does when he's in top shape. Hewitt stuck to the trail left by the horse herd and made no effort at concealment. This was the signal he had told Nico to give when he came upon the other two Americans, Peeke and Randall.

The horses had gone on, and Nicolas had already turned them to head straight north. The lad was standing beside his horse, smoking a cigarette, when Hewitt reined in. He was perhaps four miles ahead of the carriage by then.

The two dejected members of the guardia gringo sat on the damp ground. The furtive-faced Randall, who had shot the policeman yesterday, had his boots off and was stroking his tender feet. Peeke, the biggest of the four, and probably the toughest in a fight, simply sat there with a sullen, adenoidy scowl on his bearded face. Neither man was armed.

Nothing, Hewitt reflected as he pulled Coco in and dismounted, made a man look as foolish in this country as an empty holster. "Well," he said, "you boys played hell, didn't you?"

"How'd we play hell?" Peeke growled.

"You lost the horses. You got Mose hanged. You sat there like jackasses and let two files of troops trot in—*trot* in, by God!—and steal you blind. Tell me one thing you did right."

Peeke shot to his feet with a nimbleness surprising in a

man of his bulk. "Don't you git on my tail, now, Mr. Hewitt," he said. "What the hell else could we do?"

"You could have scattered the herd and rode like hell. Nobody could have caught you, the way you were mounted."

Randall slipped on his boots and stood up, too. They looked at each other and then, in embarrassment, at Hewitt.

"You just took orders, didn't you?" Hewitt said. "You did what George Boney told you to do, didn't you?"

"Well, now," Randall said, "you cain't hardly blame George. It was that kid, Mose, that made the colonel mad. *He* tried to scatter the herd, and it got his ass strung up."

"It was too late by then," Hewitt said, "but at least he had the guts to try. Tell me what happened. I want to know in your own words."

He questioned them carefully and, as he had expected, learned nothing. Their story supported Boney's. He got the impression, mostly from what Peeke said, that they had not been present while Boney was negotiating—if you could call it that—with Colonel Domínguez. Hewitt did not press it. If Boney had double-crossed them in making his deal, whatever it was, it would dawn on them sooner or later.

Hewitt called Nicolas aside and talked to him in low-voiced Spanish. Neither Randall nor Peeke spoke more than a few words of the language, but what Hewitt wanted was to impress on them that he did not trust them. Let them understand that from now on they would be merely tolerated for the work he could get out of them.

"There's grub and drinking water in the carriage," he told them when he had finished with Nicolas. "Nico will take you back and see that you're fed. You and George and Orv can ride on top of the carriage, at least for a while. They're carrying rifles. There's another one in the luggage boot. If you get any ambitious ideas, any of you, just do whatever you think you can get away with," he told them.

"Mr. Hewitt," Randall said, "you got us all wrong. Maybe we should've scattered that herd. Things look different when you're there, though."

"We're both here now. Make yourselves useful and I'll see that you're paid in full."

"Somebody," Peeke said, "ort to pay for my saddle. It cost me forty dollars in Santa Fe less'n a year ago."

"We'll see."

Hewitt started to mount. "Mr. Hewitt," Randall said, "what're you figgerin' to do? You show up in Reynosa, you might as well stand Don Aristide up against a wall and shoot him down yourself."

"We won't go to Reynosa."

"You sure as hell won't git across the river no place else."

"We'll see." Hewitt swung up into the saddle. "Maybe you had better stay with the señor and his family," he said to Nicolas, in Spanish, "and send your man on to help with the horses. What do you think?"

Nicolas merely nodded. Aristide liked and trusted him and had never abused him. But neither had he ever asked his opinion, and this was a smart kid. Smarter than Mose Kirk had been, and a lot tougher.

Hewitt turned Coco and headed toward the river. He was pretty sure that Peeke and Randall knew more than they had told him. Their suspicions of Boney had not yet had time to grow to conviction, and they were both the

kind you could pound over the head until they were dead
without ever beating a word out of them.

No, he thought, let them do some more thinking. Let
them whisper and argue with Boney. Let Peeke learn to
regret his fine saddle and Randall his sore feet a little
more poignantly. Let them all get across the river—and
then let Boney try to get away from them.

He caught up with the herd shortly. Old José, who
knew the river, and who was in charge until Nicolas returned, had left the others to hold the horses while they
grazed. He had ridden on ahead to reconnoiter both the
trail ahead and the river itself. Hewitt rode from man to
man, passing greetings and making friends. He had
learned long ago that, in this kind of job, you never could
tell when your life was going to depend on a friend.

It was almost an hour before José returned. He was too
dignified an old man to show his glee, but his eyes gave
him away.

"It is as I told you," he said in Spanish.

"I think you are an old fox," Hewitt replied in the same
language. "Very well, get the horses over, and be ready,
then, to come help us when I signal. Two shots, and then
after a brief moment, two more."

"*Sí, señor.*"

So far, so good, but they could run out of time any minute. Hewitt waited, however, until they had gotten the
herd moving at a run toward the river. Coco wanted to
run with them. Had Hewitt turned back toward the carriage sooner, the herd might have tried to follow.

Again he gave Coco his head. He had long ago learned
not to tighten up as he approached a showdown, but it
was hard not to, this time. When you had three women
on your hands, one heavy with child and one an unrelia-
bly hotheaded brat used to screaming orders and being
obeyed, you stretched the odds considerably.

CHAPTER NINE

They were less than two miles from the river when Hewitt saw one of Nicolas's men riding back toward them. Hewitt rode ahead to meet him. Nicolas had sent him back to say that once again they had intercepted the trail of the horse herd taken by Colonel Domínguez.

Hewitt rode ahead to see for himself. José had already pushed the herd across the river and they had vanished on the American side. Nicolas was waiting, slouched in the saddle, a cigarette dangling from a corner of his mouth. He did not say a word, but his gestures said plenty.

Colonel Domínguez had made a beeline for Reynosa, until he was just south of this ford. He then had turned and run the horses hard for the river, before last night's rain had hit. Some of his men had gone across with the horses, but some had also returned. The hard rain had wiped out so much sign that it was hard to tell.

"You have no feeling of surprise?" Nicolas asked in Spanish, with a hint of a smile.

"No, and neither do you."

Nicolas shrugged. It was clear that the colonel had gone into business for himself. His regiment would, no doubt, end up with the horses. But they would be paid for by government funds, at an exorbitant price, and

would be none the worse for their gallop across the ford
here and their orderly trot back across the bridge at
Reynosa.

And whatever Texas horse broker had been scouting
horses for Domínguez's regiment would honor the ancient
practice that had been followed by remount systems since
the Romans first put their Legionaires on horses. A little
gift for the commanding officer, a few odds and ends to
be passed out to his lucky troopers, and everyone was
happy.

Hewitt rode back to meet the carriage. It was midafter-
noon by now, and hot again, but not the humid, choking
heat of yesterday. Aristide called to the coachman to stop
and rest the horses. He got out and helped his wife and
daughter out, to stretch themselves after the long and
tiring ride. The maid, Socorro, remained stolidly in the
carriage.

"Have you any idea, Jeff, how we're going to cross the
river?" Aristide asked.

"Ford it," Hewitt said.

"With the carriage, too?" Aristide cried.

"We'll have to unload the luggage and carry it across.
It would help if you could ride, too, Aristide. The less
weight we have, the easier it will be."

"But my God, after last night's rain—!"

Hewitt grinned at him. "The river is probably still
booming between here and the Gulf, but there was no
rain to the west of us. José said the water would be low
here, and it is. The horses are already across."

"I can ride, too," said Josefina. "So can Socorro."

"I'll take you up on that," Hewitt said, smiling, "but I
think Socorro should ride with *la señora*, don't you? It
could be a rough crossing."

"*Como quiere,*" the girl said: Whatever you wish . . .

She was not as listless as she had been yesterday, but she was still on her best behavior.

They got back into the carriage and pushed on to the river. Here it widened, in low water, to a series of sluggish creeks divided by sandbars and, Hewitt suspected, patches of quicksand. It was an old crossing place, the banks on both sides worn down by countless herds and many a wheeled vehicle.

Nicolas sent one of his men to wade across to demonstrate the safest route. The luggage was unloaded. Once Aristide saw how shallow the water was—nowhere was it more than hip-deep—he declined to ride. He picked up two big suitcases and led the way across on foot.

Nicolas dismounted and helped Josefina up into the saddle. She hiked up her skirts to straddle it, exposing without embarrassment her shapely, tawny legs. She rode across, dismounted, and let one of Nicolas's men lead the horse back. There she stood, with her father, watching the preparations for bringing over the carriage.

The teams were unhitched and driven across the river. The carriage was rolled down the bank, restrained by brute strength of the men clustered around it. Boney, Honeycutt, and Randall, who had the captured Mausers, leaned them against a rock, freeing their hands in order to help muscle the carriage down.

All of Nicolas's men tied their ropes together and stretched them across the river. One end was tied to the eye in the carriage tongue—the other was hitched to the double trees of the wheel team and then run between them to the double trees of the leaders.

"Quick, Jeff!" Aristide called suddenly from the United States side. "Better abandon the carriage. Here come porfirista troops."

Hewitt raced back up the bank. It was a small file of

men on tired, shambling horses, too far away to be recognized. But he was sure that Captain Martínez had stayed doggedly on their trail and was ready to have another go at them.

Boney, Honeycutt, and Randall had run to snatch up their rifles. "No," Hewitt told them, "I want you to help get the carriage across. Give your guns to those fellows there."

Nicolas and two of his men took the rifles. "Don't shoot to kill," Hewitt warned them. "Keep them back until we're safely across, that's all. Only if they fire at the carriage are you to shoot to kill."

The little file of soldiers fanned out to close in on them from all sides. Hewitt gave his orders. The carriage teams, across the river, merely kept the slack out of the ropes, while the men surrounding the carriage rolled it down to the water's edge. Here Hewitt stopped them.

"Once she goes in," he said, "don't let go of it, don't ever stop, keep it rolling. If it tips over, I'm going to have somebody's hide a strip at a time."

"You expect us to git down there and wade acrost? We been afoot so long we're like to keel over. Let somebody else git wet," Boney said.

Hewitt drew his .45 and pulled back the hammer. "One more word, one false move, out of you," he said, "and I guarantee you'll keel over, Boney. Let's go!"

He gave the signal to the coachman, who put his teams in motion. The rope came taut. The carriage rolled down into water that came up to its floorboards, the men moving with it. The carriage tilted perilously, but one sharp word from Hewitt and it became level again.

It crossed the first channel and picked up speed as it rolled across the first sandbar. Into the water it went again. By now the two teams, on the American bank, were climbing steeply. They reached the top and found firmer footing.

The wet ropes snapped taut again. Again the carriage picked up speed. Two of the men—Randall and one of the Mexican guards—went down in the water. No one stopped to help them up, but when Hewitt shouted at them, both floundered after the carriage.

Hewitt kept close behind it, almost holding his breath. He heard one of the rifles boom, and then the other.

The carriage reached the United States side. The ropes were untied, and the two teams brought back to the riverside and hitched to the carriage. The sodden men again surrounded it, to keep it on its wheels by sheer brute strength as the four horses hauled it up the steep, rough bank.

Now Hewitt could see the horse herd, grazing peacefully less than half a mile away. He sent one of Nicolas's men to José with orders to cut out fourteen head and bring them back.

Aristide's wife had stepped out of the carriage, and this time the maid got out too. Hewitt waved to Nicolas, who was still standing off the soldiers, to hold their ground a little longer. In a few moments, the little bunch of horses detached from the herd came running toward them.

"You mean to turn them over to those bandits?" Aristide asked.

"You called them bandits," said Hewitt, "not I."

You did not have to draw pictures for Nico. He saw the horses coming and knew what it meant. He and his men helped haze them up the bank and start them, at a hard run, toward the soldiers. There was a moment of confusion as the incredulous soldiers almost let the horses get away. Hewitt could hear Captain Martínez shouting orders, calling his men in.

Back came the horses, heading for the river and their comrades again. Nico tossed his rifle to one of his men and headed them smartly. The soldiers managed to form a line, and several uncoiled ropes from their saddles. There was only one place the horses could cross the river, and Nicolas could hold it alone.

His two men retreated slowly, carrying all three rifles. Nico was defenseless now, except for the .45 in his holster. The soldiers closed in slowly. Nico rode like a fool as the horses broke again and again for the ford.

A rope snaked out and circled a horse's head. The soldier dallied the rope on his saddle horn and tumbled out of the saddle. His exhausted horse put its head down and braced its feet, doing its best to hold the captive. Hand over hand, the soldier walked up the rope to where he could get his hand on the horse's ear.

The horse went up on his hind legs, taking the soldier with him. When he came down, the soldier caught enough slack with his left hand to throw a half-hitch around its nose.

Now he had a crude hackamore on the horse. One of his comrades flipped a short loop with the consummate artistry that marked these Mexican riders, all of them. He caught the horse by a hind foot but did not throw him. He merely pulled his rope taut and held the horse stretched between his mount and that of the man who had roped this one.

Another horse went down, with two ropes on him, and then another. By then, the first soldier had transferred both saddle and bridle to the first horse roped. Aristide watched raptly. A splendid horseman himself, there was nothing he enjoyed more than an exhibition of horsemanship.

He saw one now. Obviously the horse had never been

ridden before, and the Mexican soldier had no time to fool around with it. He never let the horse get its head down to buck. He drove in the spurs and sent it bounding away out of sight in powerful, jackrabbit leaps. When he came back a few minutes later, the horse knew who was boss.

It took forty minutes, by Hewitt's watch, to rope twelve horses and reduce them to something like docility. The other two were roped to be led. The soldiers' own gaunt horses, grateful to be eased of their burdens, began wandering down to the river to drink.

Hewitt ordered Nico to let them drink and then get them started back to where they had come from. Captain Martínez had gotten his eleven men into a ragged line. He left them and fought his horse closer to the river. He ignored Nicolas except to hold his hand up, palm outward, in the traditional sign of peace. Hewitt mounted Coco and rode down to the water's edge on the American side.

"Thank you for a gallant act," the captain called, "but this does not end it."

"I hardly expected it would, sir," Hewitt replied.

"I call upon you to surrender Señor Castañeda to me, and the other horses likewise. The women may go free. President Díaz does not make war on women."

"You must do your duty," said Hewitt, "and I must do mine. I will return your rifles now, too, sir, but I hope it is not necessary to say that I do not expect them to be used to fire across this river."

"God damn it, Mr. Hewitt," Boney said in a low, furious voice, "you ain't going to give up them rifles. We need them."

"Maybe you do," said Hewitt, "but we don't. I'll let

you do the honors yourself. Take them over and stack them at the top of the bank."

"You mean—wade that river ag'in?"

"I mean wade that river again."

Boney looked at Aristide, who merely raised his eyebrows, as though to say, What can I do? He looked at his comrades, Honeycutt, Peeke, and Randall. They declined to meet his eyes.

"Let's hop to it," Hewitt said. "Mind you don't get those guns wet."

Boney picked up the three rifles and started across, carrying them cradled in both arms. Hewitt saw that he was heading into deep water. So did Nicolas, who called a warning.

The water was suddenly up to Boney's belt. He stopped, frightened and bewildered. "Let Nicolas help you," Hewitt called to him. "Nico, *tira la soga.*"

Nicolas flipped his rope, using only his wrist. The loop settled around Boney's body. Nicolas edged his horse upstream. Boney leaned back on the rope and let it pull him to shallower water.

He made it to the other bank, stood the rifles butt-down on the bank, and tilted their muzzles together. Nicolas motioned to him to take hold of his horse's tail to cross the stream again. He came across easily. They watched as Martínez sent three of his men to pick up the rifles. They had to fight their horses every inch of the way, and then fight to mount up again with the rifles. But they did it.

Martínez gave an order. He led off at the head of his little column, with five of his men behind him. The others rounded up their tired old horses before bringing up the rear. Hewitt took note that all three of the rifles were carried by the rear guard. Martínez might appreciate gallantry in an adversary, but he took no chances.

"They may be bandits," Aristide sighed, "but how they can ride!"

"That's your country's uniform they're wearing," Hewitt replied.

Helen and Josefina both looked up with identical expressions of surprise, and perhaps a little alarm. Aristide narrowed his eyes.

"What do you mean by that, Jeff?"

"Exactly what I say. I've brought you across the river to the United States, as I promised. I'll take you to Corpus Christi, because that's part of the contract Conrad made. But I think Martínez is a patriot, and I resent having him called a bandit. Sorry, Aristide, but that's how I feel."

"You call that a uniform," Josefina said hotly. "Good God, those filthy cotton rags are a disgrace."

"You just bet they are," Hewitt snapped, "but it's all your country can afford, and those men wear them with distinction. Mexico needs schools, more food crops, railroads, and above all, peace. If those men in those rags can pacify it, then I think it ill becomes a rich man to ridicule them as he takes his wealth to safety outside of his own country."

"By God, Hewitt," Aristide said in a quivering voice, "I've heard enough of that. You were hired to do a job, not given liberty to be insulting."

"Don't make comments to me," Hewitt said, "and expect me to keep my comments to myself. I'll tell you again, I'm not proud of the job I've done here."

"Where are my other horses?" Aristide cried. "They crossed the river here, too. Was it patriots who took them, too?"

"I wasn't there. You gave the orders that lost those horses, not I. Tell me one thing, Aristide. You had been served with an order to deliver your horses to the government, had you not? That's why you were so anxious to get them across the river. Not because you needed the money for them—only because you did not want your own government to have them!"

"I have known Porfirio Díaz for twenty-five years. He is an uncivilized brute who—"

"Stop, stop, stop this!" Josefina broke in. "He's right, Father, and you know it."

"Be quiet!" Aristide snapped.

"I shall not be quiet! You got Mose hanged. *You* can marry an American, but I can't. He's too poor, he's dirt beneath your feet, isn't he? Well, Father, I hope I'm carrying his baby. How would you like that, to have his baby for a grandchild?"

Aristide struck her across the mouth with the back of his hand. He would have slapped her again, but his own wife came between them.

"No, Aristide," she said softly but firmly. "That will settle nothing." She tried to put her arms around Josefina. "Come, child, into the carriage. No more hard words, please, please!"

"I'm not a child," Josefina said defiantly, "and I mean it, I hope I'm carrying his baby. If I'm not, it's not for lack of trying."

But she let Helen lead her to the carriage and put her inside. Helen climbed in with her. Aristide took off his hat and wiped his face with a handkerchief that was almost black with dust.

"I need a shave," he said in the voice of a man whose mind is a thousand miles away.

"You do indeed," said Hewitt.

Aristide seemed to wake up from a bad dream, with its memory still bitter in his waking mind. "I need to do some thinking, Mr. Hewitt."

"You do indeed," Hewitt said again. "Will you want me to help you to Corpus Christi?"

Aristide closed his eyes, as though to shut out from his view everything unpleasant. "Of course," he said, opening them. "Let us stay as close to the river as is safe. I wish to stop in Brownsville before going on to Corpus Christi."

"It would be shorter and safer to cut straight across to Corpus Christi."

"We will follow the river to Brownsville, and then go up the Gulf coast to Corpus Christi, if you please."

Aristide stumbled as he got into the carriage and sat beside his wife. Hewitt gave the necessary orders. The four Americans again climbed to the top of the carriage. Nicolas sent a man to tell José to move parallel to the river and close enough to keep in touch, but far enough away to keep the herd from being spotted by troops on the Mexican side.

When the coachman started the team, the sun was falling rapidly at their backs. Nicolas and one of his men fell in behind the carriage. Hewitt again took his place at its side, but did not ride as close to it as he had before.

Aristide, he noticed, was sharing a seat with Socorro, the maid, riding backward. Helen, his wife, had taken Josefina into her arms and was holding the girl tightly against the rock and jolt of the carriage. All of the resistance seemed to have gone out of Josefina.

Hewitt was aware that Boney was trying to catch his eye. He ignored the American completely, having more serious crises on his mind. He had made the mistake of going to Mexico with a short supply of cigars, counting on buying some good ones there. The chance had never come, and now he had only two left.

It was time for one now, he decided. He took it from his pocket, stroked it lovingly before putting it in his mouth, and savored the smell of the fine tobacco before lighting it. For some reason, the delicious smoke failed to fill him with the feeling of well-being that it usually brought, and this was a bad sign. Damn it, he thought, Conrad and I are going to settle a few things one of these days. No more of these impossible jobs, where everything you do is the wrong thing. . . .

CHAPTER TEN

Fatigue caught up with Hewitt about sundown, and he was glad to find a camping place. It was a cattle camp that had grown into a substation of a big cattle ranch, the John McAllen property, to the north. There was a married foreman whose chief duty was to keep cattle from being run across the Rio Grande. He was short of hands, and he looked enviously at the four Americans on Aristide's payroll.

"You wouldn't like them," Hewitt said, "but you can have them if you can hire them."

"What's wrong with them?"

"They'll sell you out first chance they get. And to jump ahead to your next question—I'll be rid of them as soon as I get the answer to a question about the last time they sold me out."

There was room in the house for Helen and Josefina, but the maid had to sleep on a quilt on the porch, and Aristide had to camp with his crew. He was coldly courteous to Hewitt. He made a point of eating by himself when the ranch foreman's wife brought out their supper, and afterward, he slept in the carriage.

The four Americans approached Hewitt as he was making his bed. He had ordered Nicolas to turn in early, too,

leaving José in command of the early watch. There was a
tree-shaded horse tank set in the fence of a corral here, so
that livestock could be watered from either side. It was
supplied by a windmill-powered pump and the overflow
had watered a little orchard. Hewitt had chosen to sleep
under a big peach tree that had just finished bearing.

Nicolas had spread his lone blanket forty feet away,
and Hewitt thought he had already fallen asleep. But as
the four Americans approached, Hewitt, out of the corner
of his eye, saw Nicolas roll over onto his left side and take
his .45 from under his blanket.

"What'll it be, boys?" Hewitt asked civilly.

"Well, Mr. Hewitt," Boney said, "the boys and me was
wonderin' what your plans are for tomorry."

"Why, push on to Brownsville."

Boney hesitated, scratching his bearded jaw. "Yes, but
you don't figger on us ridin' on top of the carriage again,
do you?"

Hewitt baited the man a little. "Where else? Do you
want to walk? You lost your horses and saddles—I didn't."

"Well, but them Mexican hands has got saddles, and
they's plenty of horses. We're top hands, Mr. Hewitt, and
it's hard lines to ride like a bunch of pilgrims in our own
country."

"Sorry, boys. Nico and his men are Don Aristide's family guard. You can't ask me to take their horses away from
them, now, can you? We've got to be fair, haven't we?
You wouldn't like it if I dismounted you to give them
your horses, after they had lost the ones they had."

Boney turned on his heel and stalked away through the
gathering darkness. The other three followed him, but
they all gave Hewitt apologetic looks that Boney would
not have liked, had he seen them.

When they were gone, Nico called softly, in Spanish,

"Don't worry yourself. They will be watched." He pointed a finger at his own eye to show just how carefully he had ordered his men to watch them.

Hewitt stretched out and fell asleep immediately. His last waking awareness was of thunder rumbling again to the southwest. If the wind happened to swing to the east . . .

The next thing he knew, someone had him by the shoulder and was shaking him gently and saying, "*Señor, señor, despiértale, por favor.*" Wake up, please. . . .

Hewitt stumbled to his feet, fitting the .45 into the belt holster he had himself designed. A light drizzle was falling, and even the smudge-fires that kept away the mosquitoes had gone out. José had been squatting beside him to stir him out silently, and came to his feet at the same time.

José led the way down the corral fence to where two of his men were trying to revive Nicolas. The boy had a huge bruise on the side of his head, and the scalp had been laid open. A series of lightning winks showed Hewitt not only the cut, but, nearby on the ground, the short chunk of iron that had, probably, been the weapon.

José had come in to see what was wrong when Nicolas failed to relieve him and his riders. Hewitt's watch showed two-thirty in the morning. José had already stirred out the second watch of the Mexican horse herders.

It was they who had discovered the bodies of the two Americans. They had been brained in their blankets, no doubt with the same piece of iron—savage blows that had killed them so quickly they literally never knew what happened. They were Dugan Peeke and Blackie Randall.

The saddles of Nico's men still hung on the fence, but two of their horses were gone. Hewitt lighted a lantern and tried to follow what sign there was. The rain had washed out most of it, light as it was, but it was still pretty clear what had happened.

Last night, Boney had proposed that they make their getaway in the night, before the rain came on. Either they had tried to talk Peeke and Randall into it, and had been turned down, or they had simply murdered their comrades in their sleep. They had made too much noise trying to steal saddles, and had aroused Nicolas.

One of them had kept Nico's attention while the other hit him from behind with the chunk of iron. They had then stolen saddles and bridles from the ranch shed, but they'd taken good Mexican horses. They would be long gone by now, and there was no use in trying to follow them.

It was not even worthwhile to stir out Aristide. Hewitt told José to relieve the night herders and put someone in charge, and go to bed with his men of the first watch. José nodded, but he did not leave Nicolas's side.

Neither did Hewitt. They moved the inert boy carefully onto a blanket, then four of them carefully carried him to the shelter of the peach tree and gently laid him down. Hewitt sent one man for a pail of cold water from the well, and he used one of his own handkerchiefs to bathe the boy's forehead and face.

The rain came down harder just before daylight. José and one of his men rigged a shelter from Hewitt's waterproof to keep the rain off Nicolas. Hewitt saw men coming out of the bunkhouse to the corrals. He left José to care for Nicolas and went to talk to the hospitable foreman who had let them camp here.

"Better count your saddles and bridles," he said. "I've got some dead men, and a couple of missing ones. Two missing horses, too."

The two missing saddles were good ones; obviously, Boney and Honeycutt had done their choosing while daylight remained. Hewitt told the foreman that they would be paid generously for the missing property, and he asked the man not to let the women know that anything was wrong.

"They've had a hard trip," he said. "Let them sleep as late as possible, and then eat a hearty breakfast. I hope there's a place we can bury these two men before it gets too light."

"We got a graveyard here," the foreman said, "naturally, but I don't know as I care much about having this kind of riffraff buried there. If what you told me about them is true, Mr. Hewitt—"

"They weren't much," Hewitt conceded, "but they were the pick of the bunch, and they're dead. I'm thinking mainly of the womenfolk, getting the job done before they wake up. We had a man hanged day before yesterday. We have had too much of this."

The rain stopped. The foreman showed them where to dig the two graves and gave them shovels that made the work go fast. Before they were finished, José came to say that he thought Nicolas had died, too. He had simply stopped breathing, without ever opening his eyes.

They dug a third grave, and this time Hewitt thought it was important that Aristide be awakened. The rancher dressed in the carriage and threw a cape over his shoulders, to kneel in the sandy mud to say the prayers over the three graves.

The foreman's wife rang the breakfast bell as they came back from the graveyard, which lay behind the little orchard. Aristide fell in beside Hewitt. He seemed to want to speak, but he was not sure where he stood with Hewitt.

"The main thing," Hewitt said, "is to get you to Brownsville as fast as we can now. I'm going to ask you to let me leave you there."

"To go after George Boney?" said Aristide. "I'm not surprised, Jeff, but it's not necessary. That's not part of your job. I'll offer a suitable reward, enough to have every peace officer in Texas on the alert."

"Please don't," said Hewitt, "and I'm not going after Boney. Orval Honeycutt's the man I want."

"What! But Honeycutt is nobody, a weakling. I am sure Boney's the vicious one."

"Exactly. He couldn't get away from all three of them, so he needed Honeycutt to help him kill the others and make off with the horses. But he'll ditch him as soon as he safely can, and leave him so scared he won't go after him. But I can do business with Honeycutt," Hewitt said grimly.

"I don't understand," Aristide said in bewilderment.

"Don't you see? Boney made a deal with Colonel Domínguez for your horses. Part of it was that their own horses, saddles, and bridles would be taken, to make it look good. I think all of them realized, by the time we got over the river, that Domínguez had left them holding the bag," Hewitt said.

"Boney's the only one with the guts to go after Domínguez and try to squeeze some money out of him. I think we're going to find that he knew Domínguez before he went to work for you. He'll know where to find him—certainly he's not going to take on his whole regiment of cavalry. I don't imagine Domínguez is worrying very much about the four American thieves that he double-crossed.

"But he should be. I can tell you this—Orv Honeycutt never had the guts to beat three men's brains in. Boney

did that. There's the man Colonel Domínguez has to deal
with now."

"He must be crazy."

"Yes," said Hewitt. "Any killer, I've found, has a streak
of madness in him. You can't anticipate what they'll do
because they don't think the way we do. That's one of the
things that make them dangerous."

The breakfast bell rang the last call. They saw the cow-
boys trooping toward the house.

"I couldn't eat a thing," said Aristide.

"Yes, you can," said Hewitt, "and you must. I don't
want the women to know about this until we're well away
from here. They've had all they can stand."

Aristide turned to face him. "Jeff, we do not see eye to
eye on some things, but I wish I could depend on you to
see us to Corpus Christi. This other thing—Boney—can
wait, can't it?"

"No."

Aristide squinted at him. "Mose Kirk? Jeff, vengeance
is the most profitless thing in the world."

"Perhaps," said Hewitt, "but when I make a mistake, I
square it. When you come right down to it, my reputation
is my second gun."

"The Hewitt legend."

"If that's what you want to call it. People know I live
up to my word, back up my men, stand by my friends—
and never give up on my enemies."

Aristide laid his hand on Hewitt's shoulder. "It is hard
to say this, *amigo*, but you are not doing this for Josefina's
sake?"

"No."

They began walking toward the house, to help bring
the breakfast out to their crew. "I think I could have
stood anything," Aristide said. "Loss of my rancho, my

eminence as one of Mexico's leaders—but the world
seemed to come to an end when my daughter said what
she said yesterday. What am I to do if she does have
Mose Kirk's child?"

"That," said Hewitt, "is your problem."

They were on the way in an hour, leaving behind
friends they could count on. Aristide paid handsomely for
the stolen saddles and bridles, for the food they had
eaten, and for the inconvenience they had caused. He was
at his winning and most charming best—and Aristide Castañeda López, as Hewitt already knew, could be a
charmer.

The women did not seem to notice that the four Americans were not with them, and that Nicolas, too, was missing. Hewitt left it up to Aristide to tell them. It was going
to be hot again today, and humid. He meant to make no
more mistakes and to lose neither men nor horses. He was
not sure that old José had either Nicolas's gift of command or his sense of responsibility, and from now on until
they reached Brownsville, he meant to run this job down
to the most minute detail.

CHAPTER ELEVEN

Four days later they pulled into Brownsville, near the mouth of the Rio Grande and the Gulf of Mexico. It had rained every day without ever cooling off much, and the nights had been hot. Horse-killing weather it was, and the heavy carriage, even with extra teams, gaunted the horses swiftly.

Brownsville was a busy town, a rowdy town, a wide-open town that today was full of blue-clad cavalrymen. Hewitt saw an officer he knew, Major Lafayette "Lafe" Wisdom. Lafe was standing on the sidewalk in front of the best saloon in town, talking with some local businessmen. A short, burly, energetic man who had risen to the rank of major general in the Civil War, he had grown gray in the service without losing any of his enthusiasm for life.

He did not see Hewitt, who pulled Coco through the mud almost to the sidewalk where the three men stood talking. He stopped the big stallion quietly.

"I can whip any three officers in the whole Seventh Cavalry," he said loudly.

Wisdom jumped as though someone had jabbed him with a pin from behind. His squarish, clean-shaven face turned a fiery red, and he squared his shoulders and closed both fists.

Then his jaw dropped. "Hewitt, you damned scoundrel, if this isn't a coincidence!" he shouted, leaning out over the mud to shake hands. "There's been a fellow here looking for you the last few days."

"Who?" Hewitt leaned out to clasp the officer's hand.

"I don't know. Some kind of a Dutchman. He's buying the beer pretty freely, and asking about you. Tie that beautiful jumping-horse of yours and I'll buy one for you."

"I can't," Hewitt said, "but I'll see you later."

"Where'll you be, if this fellow is still looking for you?"

"I don't know, and neither do you. Suppose you let me find him."

Wisdom grinned. "Same old Hewitt. But you look like hell, you know."

"I feel like hell," Hewitt said.

He gave Wisdom a wave that was half salute and trotted Coco after the carriage. Aristide obviously knew where he was going. The trail-wise horse herd followed close behind the carriage, bringing stares of admiration from everyone on the street, especially the cavalrymen.

They turned north, no doubt on the road to Corpus Christi, and at the edge of town Aristide stopped the carriage to give José orders. Hewitt did not bother to listen, but he saw Aristide point to a brick house that stood, surrounded by trees and corrals, not far north of town. José sent one man on ahead, and after a moment followed him with the herd.

When the herd had passed, the coachman started his tired teams. Hewitt dropped in behind the carriage and got out his last cigar. He saw the horses headed, saw them shunted swiftly down the fenced side road to one of the corrals behind the brick house.

The carriage turned down the same road, Hewitt keeping a rod or two behind. An attempt had been made to grow a little grass in front of the house, but it had been grazed off. The carriage stopped at a side entrance.

Behind the house stood a crude pergola. Over the rough-lumber latticework of the sides and roof, wild grapes had grown profusely. An old Mexican was grubbing away at the grass that was encroaching upon the roots of the grapes. A hen with new chicks at her side waited to dart in and snatch the insects turned up by the old gardener. She was a tall, brawny game-chicken, red and black and gold in color—the mother of champion fighters, Hewitt would have bet.

A man came out of the pergola, holding a book and blinking in the bright sunlight. He was of average height, squarely built, and even in this oppressive heat was dressed with a formality strange to this country. He wore a checked suit with a red-piped, fawn-colored weskit, and a maroon necktie was tied in a neat knot at his stiff celluloid collar. On his feet were freshly blacked boots with flat heels—on his head, a derby hat—on his nose, a haughty pince-nez attached to a fine gold chain.

Hewitt swung down from the saddle and walked toward him, leading his horse. "I'll be go to hell, Conrad," he said. "You're a few blocks off your beat, aren't you?"

"Good day, Jefferson," said his partner, Conrad Meuse. "You are late. You were to have been in Corpus Christi by now."

They did not shake hands. It was always a pleasure to Hewitt to see his partner, but they had never been demonstrative friends. Besides, they had always maintained a neat division of duties, and he did not particularly care to have Conrad interfering with his work in the field.

An old Mexican woman hurried to open the door of the carriage. The maid got out first and assisted Helen out. Next, Josefina came down slowly, wearily, taking no interest in where she was. It was impossible for Hewitt to detect if she had ever been here before.

Aristide got out, hand extended. "Conrad!" he cried. "So nice to see you. May I present my wife and my daughter. This roughneck of course you already know."

Conrad bowed deeply. Aristide's wife gave him her hand. After a moment, Josefina did likewise, but she seemed to be sleepwalking. Her expression did not change, and she acknowledged the introduction with a mere nod.

Aristide gave orders in Spanish to the two servants. He called the gardener to come carry in the luggage and told the coachman to put the horses up. He held the door open while the two serving women carried in the little vanity cases that both Helen and Josefina had with them.

"They will show you to your rooms, my dears," he said. "Mr. Meuse and Jeff and I must have a little talk. I believe the pergola is the most comfortable place."

Hewitt said nothing. Aristide and Conrad paid each other extravagant compliments as they walked back to the pergola and chose chairs.

"You're looking extraordinarily well, Aristide."

"I'm a disgrace. How I'll enjoy a bath and a shave and fresh linen! You seem to get younger every time I see you, Conrad."

"That's an illusion. It's a reflection of your own imperishable youth."

"Youth! I wish I had yours. I should not then have been such a burden to friend Hewitt."

Aristide and Conrad took comfortable cowhide chairs in the shade of the grapevines. Hewitt, his impatience rising, along with his suspicion, merely took off his hat and leaned against the framework of the pergola, crossing his ankles.

Conrad took a box of six cigars from his coat pocket. "Your brand, my dear Jeff, and quite fresh."

Hewitt selected a cigar, bit off the end, and lighted it. "All right, Conrad, what's it all about? Whatever it is you're planning, I'm not going to do it."

"You tell him, Aristide," said Conrad.

Aristide beamed. "I want you to go on to Corpus Christi with me, and then on to New York with Conrad while he conducts some business for me."

Hewitt held up his hand. "Nothing doing," he said before Aristide could go on. "I told you what I'm going to do now. One night's sleep, and I'm off."

Conrad cocked his left eyebrow. "What kind of nonsense is this, Jefferson? Off to where?"

"On the trail of a murderer," Aristide said. "A bad one, I acknowledge. I shall offer a reward of five thousand dollars for his capture. That's enough to ensure that someone will either arrest him or kill him, surely."

"No, I'm going after him myself. I told you why."

"But, Jeff, everything is relative. This man—"

"There's nothing relative about him," Hewitt cut in. "He is my number-one task, until further notice."

"Whom did he murder?" Conrad asked quietly.

Hewitt deferred to Aristide with an angry little nod. Aristide winced as he told about the hanging of Mose Kirk, and the memory of his daughter's outburst came back to him. He said nothing about that, however, but rushed on to tell of the assassination of Nicolas, Peeke, and Randall.

When Conrad became excited, he showed it only in a strong Germanic accent. "You feel this is so important?" he said, and it came out, "You pfeel dis ist tso imbordant?"

"If I didn't," Hewitt said, "I wouldn't do it."

"You feel responsible, is dat it?"

"Perhaps not that much, but the way the story will be circulated, I'll be held responsible. I can't permit that."

"I zee, I zee." Conrad frowned. "Gan you not but it off for a month?"

Hewitt did not even bother to shake his head. "The truth, I'm afraid," Aristide said, "is that he is doing it mostly for my daughter's sake. The truth is—" He dropped his eyes in shame and could not go on.

"The truth is," Hewitt finished for him, "Josefina was infatuated with him. That matters only a very small damn to me. She's a headstrong young woman who made herself an unpleasant nuisance more than once on this trip. I'm very sorry if she's unhappy but I don't regard her as a wronged woman."

"I don't understand," Conrad said.

"Mose was a pleasant-enough kid who someday might have amounted to something," Hewitt said impatiently. "Josefina gave him big ideas. She made him feel more mature than he was. My guilty responsibility is that I took him at that false self-evaluation. Had I known that they were in love, I would never have given him that job."

"You are too subtle for me," said Conrad.

"There's nothing subtle about it. I gave him a job that it took a hell of a man to do, because I thought he was a hell of a man. She had made him think he was one, too. But even that is beside the point."

He leaned forward and pointed the cigar at Conrad.

"The important thing is that I can't afford—I will not risk —having it said that I put a man in a job where he got strung up *and I did nothing about it!*"

Conrad frowned. "But the murder of this boy happened in Mexico, and this man did not do it," he said. "If you capture him in the United States, he can be punished only if you prove he murdered the other three. So even if you find him, everything is a muddle."

"I guarantee it won't be a muddle."

Conrad and Aristide looked at each other, and then Conrad hitched another cowhide chair close to them. He nodded for Hewitt to sit down. Hewitt did so. They leaned toward him and Conrad dropped his voice.

"I tell you what is more important than this, Jefferson," he said. "Den you will see dat you can do dis vun job, and take a year off to find your murderer. Aristide has with him six hundred thousand dollars' worth of unset diamonds that we must take to New York to sell to Tiffany."

Hewitt looked at Aristide. "You mean that we had six hundred thousand dollars' worth of diamonds in the carriage with us, all the way up from the rancho?"

"Yes," Aristide said smugly. "My father began collecting unset diamonds before I was born. I buy a few every year. They'll go on being the best investment in the world, over the long term. I'm sorry to part with these, but I have others. *Ai Dios,* I need money!"

Conrad tapped Hewitt's knee. "That's why it was necessary for you to escort him. Now you must go with us to Curpus Christi. There he will settle down with his family, while you and I go on to New York to sell his diamonds."

"What's the fee in it?"

"Ten per cent of anything up to six hundred thousand —twenty per cent over that."

"Fair enough," said Hewitt, "but you don't need me."

"*Mein Gott,* you are the one who knows diamonds—you are reliable gunman to make dese diamonds safe!"

"Tiffany will pay you all the diamonds are worth, and guarding them is no problem. You wear them next to your skin, and you carry a gun. If anyone tries to take them away from you, shoot him. It's really quite simple."

Conrad looked at him helplessly, Aristide with a smile of amusement. "Come, friend Hewitt," Aristide said, standing up, "come see my lovely diamonds. Do you know diamonds?"

"A little. I've worked on a couple of jewel cases."

"I wonder what there is you do not know. I wonder how one is educated to be a private detective, since a private detective has to know everything."

Aristide led the way into the house, where Helen and Josefina were drinking lemonade and eating bean burritos in the small, hot living room. Helen had learned to eat Mexican food and like it, and Josefina looked as though she did not know what she was eating.

In the small main bedroom, Aristide pulled one of his valises out from under the bed and opened it. It was one of the older pieces of luggage he had, and by far the shabbiest. From the mass of dirty clothes in it he took a heavy deerskin bag, the leather tanned with the hair on it. He smoothed the red blanket on the bed and dumped the diamonds out onto it.

"Look them over, Jeff. I have had every one of them duplicated in paste, for safety's sake. Some of the older ones, which my father bought, must be worth three or four times what he paid for them. He bought perfection rather than size, and that has been my rule, too. How much do you estimate they're worth on today's market?"

Hewitt sorted through the stones swiftly. He looked up

angrily at Aristide. "What the hell are you trying to pull on us, Aristide?" he said.

"Pull on you? What do you mean?" Aristide said stiffly. "I don't care at all for your tone, my friend."

"I don't care what you care," Hewitt said. "These would be worth close to a million dollars—*if* they were real. What kind of switch are you trying to pull on us? Where are the real stones?—if you've got any. These are paste."

CHAPTER TWELVE

Aristide looked ready to faint. The color drained from his face and he put his hand over his heart and gasped for breath. "Paste?" he said. "Paste? Impossible! I left the paste behind. My diamonds, my diamonds! These are the real ones. They must be, they must be!"

He scrambled unsteadily through the stones on the bed. He clutched two handfuls and squeezed hard, as though to put pressure on them to tell him the truth. He looked at Hewitt helplessly.

"Surely, if you've been buying diamonds for so many years, you can tell a real one from paste," said Hewitt.

"If I see them together, yes. I am not an expert. You are sure, Jeff?"

"Any country jeweler could tell you, Aristide. They're very good paste, but still paste."

"Paste?" said Conrad in bewilderment. "I have heard the term, but what does it mean exactly?"

"Glass. A form of brilliant flint glass containing some lead," Hewitt said. "It has been used to simulate diamonds for a hundred years. Glassmakers call it 'strass,' after a German by the name of Strass or Strasser who invented it a hundred years ago."

Conrad picked up one of the larger "diamonds," one

that would have weighed about ten carats—*if* it had been a diamond. "You are sure?" he asked.

"This is a disaster," Aristide said, when Hewitt only nodded. "I packed this valise myself. I myself put the false diamonds in a drawer in my office at the rancho, where the porfiristas would find them, and, perhaps, leave my other property alone. If they thought they had a fortune in diamonds of mine, would not that be enough?"

Neither Hewitt nor Conrad answered. Aristide left the paste diamonds on the bed until Hewitt himself scooped them up and put them in the deerskin bag.

"Disaster," Aristide said mournfully. "Disaster!"

"You'll starve, I suppose," Hewitt said.

"By no means. I am not a poor man, but now I must give up some very important plans."

"What plans?"

"I do not care to discuss that."

"Shall I tell you instead?" Hewitt said. "You were going to use the money from your diamonds to finance a revolution against President Díaz. You were going to try to buy off troops along the river, weren't you? Fine horses and money—that would tempt many a general! Well, I'm glad you lost your damned diamonds!"

"You are a porfirista yourself," Aristide almost shouted.

"No," said Hewitt, "and I'm not necessarily against revolutions. My own government is for Díaz. I don't know which side I'd be on, if it came to that."

He pointed his finger at Aristide. "But I'll tell you what I *won't* stand for, my friend. No man on earth can lie to me and get away with it. You claimed to be an innocent victim of persecution—all you wanted was to escape. And all the time you were plotting rebellion—all the time you involved me in it—and I only learn about it now."

"Wait one minute, both of you," said Conrad Meuse,

calmly. "You are both forgetting the important thing. Is it possible, Jefferson, to recover the diamonds?"

"I have no idea. I'm not interested."

"But a million dollars—"

"I haven't lost a million dollars, and I'm not going to lose a minute's sleep because Aristide has."

"Please, friend Hewitt," said Aristide, "put your mind to work. I am like a steer stunned by the hammer of the butcher. Tell me what I am to do."

"First," said Hewitt, "sell those damned horses. They're going to be a temptation to every thief and bandit on both sides of the border. Forget revolution! With your diamonds gone, you're not going to have one anyway. I tell you this, so long as you own those horses, you're not safe here. Many a man has been killed for *one* such horse, and you have thirty-one."

Aristide gripped his hands together, nodding. "I can use the money. Could you sell them for me, friend Hewitt? And then get me safely to Corpus Christi with my family?"

"Once you're rid of the horses," Hewitt said, "there'll be less reason for some hothead to assassinate you. José can get you to Corpus Christi."

"You will not escort us there?"

"I told you, I'm on other duty."

"Very well," Aristide sighed, "sell the horses."

"First I want a bath, a shave, something to eat, a little sleep, time to think."

Aristide did not look happy. Conrad said, "There is nothing you can do with this stubborn man, Aristide. I will have another hammock slung in the pergola and covered with mosquito netting for him. It will go well, I think, if I for once share some of the hardships of his work."

"Hardships?" Hewitt said. "Have Aristide tell you where I slept on the way up here. A hammock in the breeze, protected from the mosquitoes—and you call that *hardship?* We must trade jobs for a while."

He took his last clean clothing from his small satchel, and bathed in icy water fresh from the well, in a tub set up next to the windmill. The old gardener brought him a big mirror, which he hung on the windmill while he shaved. By the time he got back to the pergola, Conrad had slung both covered hammocks.

"I have learned to take a nap in the afternoon, since I arrived here, Jefferson," he apologized. "I hope you will not regard it as a decadent luxury if I indulge in one now."

"I'm going to myself," said Hewitt. "Here, they're called the *siesta*, and they're a national institution."

He stretched out in the hammock, feeling clean and relaxed and at peace for the first time in more than two weeks. Conrad got into the other one. Hewitt led him to talk of Aristide Castañeda López, whom he had met in New York. "A complex and fascinating man," said Conrad. "The very image of a powerful and distinguished Indian chieftain, and yet completely European in his soul."

"I can understand that," Hewitt murmured sleepily. "How did he meet his wife?"

Her name had been Helen Richey, and her father was a small grocer on the outskirts of Washington. Rather, he had been; since his daughter's marriage, Aristide had financed a food-importing business for him. "Doing very well, too," said Conrad. "Aristide's commercial instincts were inherited from his mother's people. The López name is on banks, brokerage houses, and newspapers throughout central Mexico. I don't understand how Mexicans sign their names. His father was a Castañeda—why is he Aristide Castañeda López? And why is his daughter Josefina Castañeda Baca?"

"It's the old Spanish way." Hewitt went on to explain that a Mexican man, especially if he was proud of his maternal lineage, added his mother's maiden name to his own. A married woman retained her maiden name, adding "de" and her husband's name. "His first wife, I take it," he said, "was a Baca?"

"Yes, Maria de Asunción Baca."

"Named," said Hewitt, "in honor of the Virgin Mary, probably on the feastday of her assumption bodily into heaven. Very well, without knowing her mother's maiden name, I can't give you her complete entitlements. But after her marriage to Aristide, she would be known as Maria de Asunción Baca de Castañeda López. And Aristide's daughter, Josefina, is properly Josefina Castañeda Baca. Suppose she marries a fellow whose father's name was Ramírez and whose mother's name was de los Santos —her name properly would be Josefina Castañeda de Ramírez de los Santos."

"It is all very bewildering."

"No, if family is important to you, it's all very clear. You carry your pedigree on your calling card. I understand his first wife died."

He had Conrad safely sidetracked. "Yes," Conrad said, "when Josefina was four. It was difficult, Aristide says, for her to accept a stepmother after all those years. She absolutely refused to give Helen any respect until less than a year ago. Poor Aristide, he is so in love with Helen, and— why is this important?"

"It isn't," Hewitt lied. "You still didn't tell me how he met Helen."

"He was in Washington on business, at the embassy—

this was before he fell out with President Díaz. He stopped a runaway horse, and she was in the buggy. It was all quite gallant and brave on his part, and impossibly romantic." Conrad had no patience with romance.

"She seems to me to be a remarkable woman," Hewitt said with a yawn.

"What do you think of Josefina?"

"A brat."

"She will be a rich woman, Jefferson." Hewitt did not answer. After a moment, Conrad went on, "Aristide is upset about the diamonds, but I know he is concerned about his daughter's future. When I asked him what he thought of you, after being with you so long, he replied, 'There is the man strong enough and yet gentle enough to make my daughter happy.' I would be happy to act as marriage broker in your behalf."

Hewitt let a small snore bubble between his lips. Conrad tried again. "I have always been concerned with your tomcat ways, Jefferson. You take such risks—and besides, it can be so expensive!" He swiftly drifted out of Hewitt's consciousness as it became no longer necessary to fake a snore. The flies and mosquitoes circled the netting over Hewitt's hammock in vain, uttering frantic sounds of frustration with their busy wings. He slept.

It was almost evening when he awakened, half starved. The servants had chickens and a leg of veal roasting over coals in the backyard, but Hewitt had let his mind make itself up while he slept.

"No, I'll find a friend who can be useful in selling the horses," he said, "and I'll treat him to dinner. That's the first order of business, Conrad."

Aristide cracked his knuckles in vexation, trying to

maintain a pleasant demeanor. "You will not even try to recover my diamonds?" he said.

"Yes, but in my own way."

"After you have ferreted out this George Boney, and punished him publicly."

"I think I'll be doing both at the same time, Aristide."

"You think he got away with them?" Aristide cried.

"No, but I think he'll lead me to them. I could almost promise you that you'll have your diamonds within twenty-four hours after I get back."

"When will that be?"

"I wish I knew."

"That," Conrad said reproachfully, "is not very satisfactory, Jefferson. Why do you find it necessary to be mysterious so much of the time? You leave me in the dark on so many things! I can understand that, perhaps, when we must communicate by the telegraph wires. But when we are face to face—damn it, man, it's insulting!"

Hewitt made Conrad face him. "Have I ever lied to you?"

"No, but—"

"Have I ever failed to finish a job for you?"

"That is not the—"

"In short, have I ever let you down? Conrad, don't you believe by now that I know my job? It is necessary for me to keep certain things to myself at this time. That is all you need to know."

Conrad was still angry, but he knew better than to alienate a rich client. "There you are, Aristide," he said. "One can do nothing with this mule-headed Hewitt. Please compose yourself. You will have your diamonds back, although God knows when."

"Just don't mention them again to anyone—to *anyone*,

do you understand that? Now, there is one other thing I
want to do, while I still retain the details in my mind."

Among the native talents Hewitt had was a certain degree of skill in portraiture. He would never be an artist,
and he knew it, but he could have made his living at it
had it become necessary. He never traveled without his
crayons, which were the best money could buy, but in
somewhat sad shape now because of the long siege of in-
tensive heat.

He begged a small piece of white paper from Aristide
and on it drew a picture of George Boney. He pictured
Boney with his hat pushed back on his head, as he never
wore it, but this showed both his face and the kind of hat
he favored. Both Conrad and Aristide leaned over the
table to watch him.

"*Ai Dios*, man, you're a real artist," Aristide exclaimed.
"But you have given him too full a mouth, and it does not
show his hangdog hatred. His mouth betrays him as a
man who hates the world."

"Like this?"

"No, no, friend Jeff. The eyes are exactly right, the eyes
of a weasel, sly, and—do you mind if I try a mouth to go
with those eyes?"

Hewitt handed over the crayon. Aristide leaned over
the picture and blurred the mouth slightly with the end
of his finger. He slashed in a new mouth with short, swift
strokes, and switched crayons to change the shape of the
bearded chin. The living Boney leaped out at them suddenly from a piece of paper no more than eight inches
long and six wide.

"That's the man," said Hewitt.

"The one you're going to hunt down?" said Conrad.

Hewitt nodded. "You're the artist, Aristide," he said.

"Why have you never developed that exquisite talent? You're the best I have ever met."

"Why did you develop yours?"

"I had to. I'm a jack of all trades and master of none, but a pretty good jack because I had to be."

"And I never did. You are lucky, friend Hewitt, that life forced you to become somebody. There is nothing more despicable than a rich failure."

Conrad picked up the paper. "He is a cornered rat," he said. "Who would trust such a man with a dime?"

"Aristide did," said Hewitt. "He trusted him with his horses, his family, and his honor. And now what we've got to do is get back as much as we can of it."

CHAPTER THIRTEEN

He made a special point of telling José to keep a close
guard on the horses all night. They were in an enclosed
pasture, but a stout fence of four barbwire strands was
good protection only until someone came along with a
good pair of wirecutters. Twenty seconds—that was all it
took.

He tied Coco in the center of town, in front of the Lone
Star Saloon. The horse was sure to attract attention. If
someone took a notion to steal him, Hewitt wanted plenty
of witnesses.

He hoofed the streets, ravenously hungry, searching for
Major Wisdom. He saw plenty of cavalrymen, including a
few officers, but no Lafe. He gave up at about ten o'clock
and went into the Lone Star.

It was stiflingly hot but not crowded. He chose corned
beef and cabbage at the lunch counter, and ordered a
schooner of beer.

"You're Mr. Hewitt, aren't you?" said the bartender.

"Yes, why?"

"Saw you talkin' to Major Wisdom. Any friend of his'n
is a friend of mine. You pick a table yander, and I'll fetch
your supper to you."

"Thank you, and two fingers of your best, too."

Hewitt had to dispossess a blowsy drunk at the corner table by giving him two dimes, but here he could sit with two walls protecting his back. The bartender, balancing a big tray clumsily, brought him a plate heaped with corned beef, cabbage, and boiled potatoes, a bowl of blackberry cobbler with a pile of thick cream on it, and a big tankard of beer. There was also a bottle of whiskey and a glass.

"You're an old trooper yourself, aren't you?" Hewitt asked.

"Yes, sir, the Seventh."

"Don't 'sir' me. Two stripes was the highest I ever got." Hewitt picked up the bottle. "Where's your glass? Won't you join me?"

"Haven't tasted the stuff since I went to servin' it. Army taught me one thing, Mr. Hewitt. A man has to live by rules. Too many of 'em, and you might as well be in jail. But you got to have a few, and a man who serves out the hard stuff had better never taste it."

Hewitt would have bet that the cavalry lost a good man when this fellow decided to go into bartending. You found these restless stags everywhere, smart men, loquacious, usually uneducated, but curious, imaginative, good thinkers. This one responded with pleasure to Hewitt's invitation to sit down with him. Hewitt poured a stiff drink and raised his glass.

"To the Seventh Regiment, United States Cavalry."

"Thank you, Mr. Hewitt. Damned good outfit. Major Wisdom fit in the Seventh. Was a lieutenant then. What the hell's the matter with the Army when they let a fightin' man like him go to waste? Led a division under Grant, and then had to go back to shavetail and now he's only a goddamn staff officer."

Something was on his mind. "I've heard," Hewitt said, "that his men would follow him to hell and gone."

"Bet your goddamn life."

"Where is he tonight?"

"Who knows? When he seen them horses of yours, he wanted one so bad he could taste it. Man like him deserves a good horse, and you should see what he rides! What I'm gittin' at, Mr. Hewitt, is, how much would one of them horses cost? I might be able to stake the major to one if they don't go too high. His credit is good with me."

"Suppose you let me worry about that. If you see him, tell him I'm looking for him."

The bartender heaved a deep sigh. "Sure will. Don't you let all of them horses go without he gets one, you hear? And if there's ever anything I kin do for you—"

"There is." Hewitt took a tube of carefully rolled paper from his inside pocket, and unrolled it to expose the picture he and Aristide had drawn of George Boney. "Ever seen this man?"

The bartender studied the picture a long time before shaking his head. "No, never have. But I bet I know him if I see him in the future."

"If you do, it's worth a hundred dollars to me to know about it as soon as possible."

The bartender shook his head. "You'll hear about it. Don't you try to pay me! Time I got back to work."

Hewitt feasted at his leisure. He was almost through eating, and it was almost midnight, when the doors swung open and the short, burly form of Major Wisdom appeared. Hewitt called to him, and the officer came over, slapped his campaign hat on the table, and sat down without being invited.

"Jeff," he said, "what are you going to do with those horses?"

"Sell them."

"When?"

"As soon as possible."

Wisdom winced. "Could you hold off a couple of days?"

"Why?"

"I wired to J. Grover Todd. Know who he is?"

"Yes." Todd was a horsebroker who did business all over the southwestern states and sometimes in Mexico. He was well and favorably known to the Army Remount Service, despite having made most of his money buying for the British. On fine horses especially, they could outbid the Americans.

"Todd's got a deal," Wisdom said, "where he buys horses for officers that like to pick their own and buy them with their own money. That forty-odd head you've got might strain him a little, but he could sell every one of them in the officer corps."

"Not forty," said Hewitt. "There are an extra carriage team in that bunch, and a few my man wouldn't part with. Say twenty-eight head."

"If you don't hold him up on the price, Todd can finance that many. Can't you hold off for a few days?"

"It wouldn't be easy, Lafe. I'm in a hurry. I'm on a job that can't wait."

Wisdom could only clench his teeth and glare at him. Hewitt had met him in California when he was working a queer sort of case. A fugitive he was hunting down had taken cover, like so many, in the Army, under an assumed name. But when Hewitt caught up with him, half the regiment was down with typhoid—including the fugitive.

Wisdom had arranged for Hewitt to work in the typhoid ward for a week, until his man got well enough for him to arrest. Wisdom himself had a horror of typhoid.

For two weeks after the man had been shipped back to Phoenix in chains, to stand trial for murder, Wisdom would not let Hewitt near him.

"You may be a damn fool," he said, from a safe distance, "but I'm not, and I ain't got your kind of luck."

"It's not luck," said Hewitt. "You just don't eat anything contaminated, you drink only boiled water, and you—"

"You have luck built into you," Wisdom shouted. "You're a lucky son of a bitch, Hewitt, and luck beats boiled water anytime."

"Lafe," Hewitt said now, "I'm going to see that you get a horse you can afford. Stop worrying!"

"Yes," said Wisdom, "but how about my colonel? I talked too damn much. They all know I know you. The colonel wants to get a couple for General Harding. If General Domínguez outbids—"

"General *who?*" Hewitt cut in sharply.

"New commander in Matamoros. Just took command today, and he's got one company mounted on the most beautiful horses you ever seen. Say! Something mighty queer here. General Domínguez turns up with a whole company mounted like the kaiser's best, and the same day, here you come with a herd of the same. That didn't just happen, Jeff."

"No, it didn't," Hewitt said. "Let me think."

So Colonel Domínguez was now General Domínguez, and he had taken command in Matamoros. If George Boney had gone to Reynosa in search of Domínguez, he would soon be back here.

Hewitt found his heart beating a little faster at the thought of the two men who had been responsible for hanging Mose Kirk. The impression he had of Domínguez was not favorable—an overbearing man, cruel, with no regard for human life. Yet Hewitt could condone his part in the hanging more easily than he could Boney's. There had been at least the shadow of an excuse of military necessity. There could be none for a treacherous American civilian horse thief.

Again he took out the rolled crayon picture of Boney. "Have you ever seen this man, Lafe?"

Wisdom only glanced at it. "Sure. Can't really recall his name, but if it's important, give me time."

"George Boney."

"That's it!"

"When and where did you see him?"

Wisdom wanted to talk horses. He was brusque and to the point. "Way last spring. Was on a routine patrol over on the John McAllen ranch, near the bridge to Reynosa. Picked this fellow up with a string of horses—five or six— that he couldn't account for. Was going to turn him over to the sheriff, but he decamped over the bridge in the night. We gave the horses to the sheriff, and I guess sure enough they were stolen."

Whereupon, Hewitt had no doubt, Boney had worked his way southward, to go to work, if you could call it that, for Aristide.

"If you see him again," he said, "I want to know about it. He'll probably have another fellow with him. I want to know about him, too. Now, about these horses—"

In a horse trade, you had to set something up to shoot at and deal from there. Plucking figures out of thin air, Hewitt said he had twelve horses worth $215 each, for a total of $2,580. Another eleven were easily worth $100 each, for a total of $2,200.

"There are five," he said, "I could let go for one hundred and eighty-five each. That's nine hundred and twenty-five. The entire twenty-eight head for five thousand, seven hundred and five—say fifty-seven hundred even, to round it off."

Lafe Wisdom was a fine officer but no horse trader. He ran his hand through his hair hopelessly. "How the hell am I going to come up with that kind of money if I can't get hold of Todd? And where does that leave me? And I'll tell you this—the minute this General Domínguez hears about these horses, he's going to outbid us. I have to be honest with you, Jeff—he's got more money than we have."

Hewitt let him suffer a moment. "Tell you what I'd like to do, Lafe," he said then. "I want to get these horses off my hands. We'll go out there tomorrow and pick one out for you. Then I'm going to give you three more days to get hold of Todd—on one condition."

"What's that?"

"I want you to get those horses out of there and let the cavalry be responsible for them. If somebody hasn't come up with fifty-seven hundred dollars three days from to-morrow morning, they go to the highest bidder. How can I do more than that?"

Lafe insisted on shaking his hand over and over. "Jeff, if there's ever anything I can do for you," he said almost tearfully, "you just send up a smoke signal and I'll come. How much is my horse going to cost me, and how do I arrange to pay for him?"

"Your horse will be your fee for taking this off my hands. When can you have a detail out there to move the horse herd to your corrals?"

"Is daylight too early? Jeff, give me three days and I guarantee nobody but an American cavalry officer is ever going to own one of those horses."

They walked out together and stood on the steamy sidewalk for a moment, smoking together. Late as it was, there was still a crowd of men trudging aimlessly up and down the street, fighting mosquitoes and dreading going to bed.

A man on the other side of the street was shambling along, with his head down, his hands in his pockets. He looked around, started on, stopped suddenly, and took a second look. Coco was getting restless and anxious to get home, and had stamped the mud hard, the way a stallion will.

The man started across the street, ignoring the churned-up mud underfoot. Hewitt caught Lafe by the arm. "Sh-h!" he hissed, and pulled him back into the darkness against the wall of the Lone Star.

The man stopped halfway across the street and then turned and hurried back. He had recognized Coco, but had not picked Hewitt and Wisdom out of the crowd. And Hewitt had recognized him.

That was Orval Honeycutt, broke and despondent. If ever a man was between the devil and the deep blue sea, it was Honeycutt. He had money coming from Aristide that he dared not try to collect. He was, beyond doubt, in absolute terror of Boney, but so long as Boney needed him, he would stay with him. He *had* to stay with Boney. Besides being broke, he was weak and frightened. He was probably seeing Mose Kirk's dangling body in his nightmares.

Honeycutt went out of sight up an alley. Hewitt pointed to it. "Lafe, what's back there, do you know?"

"Town wagon lot, with a shed where jobless riders can throw their blankets down under a roof. "Why?"

"Lafe, do you know where you could get me a pair of handcuffs in a hurry—no questions asked?"

"I think I could get some from the sheriff. I know I could get some out at camp."

"The sheriff will do. I'm in a hurry. Can you get them and bring them to me?"

The puzzled officer headed for the sheriff's office. Hewitt slipped into the saloon, borrowed a piece of paper from the sleepy bartender, and wrote a note:

Conrad: This introduces Maj. Lafayette Wisdom. He will take possession of the horse herd, if I am not back by daylight. Fix it with Aristide.

He did not bother to sign it. When Wisdom returned with the handcuffs, Hewitt put them in his back pocket and put the key on his ring. He gave Wisdom the note.

"Hand this to my partner, Conrad Meuse," he said, "and not to anyone else. I'll try to be there by daylight. If I'm not, have a Spanish-speaking trooper with you who can talk to José, the man in charge of the herd. He's to hold back the carriage teams, help you take your pick of what's left, and then turn over to you thirty-two of what remains."

"You better be there," Wisdom said doubtfully. "Where'll you be, if you're not?"

"You don't want to know that, Lafe," said Hewitt.

CHAPTER FOURTEEN

The mud in the alley had dried out just enough to cling, making it difficult to walk quietly. It was so dark that Hewitt had to feel his way along the side of a building until, suddenly, a glimmer of light appeared as he came to the wagon lot. A coal-oil lantern hung on a nail in the open shed that Lafe Wisdom had described.

In its dim light he could count nine sleeping men, none of whom looked like the one he was seeking. There was only one wagon on the lot, but more than a dozen tied horses were feeding on both sides of a hay feeder near the shed.

He stopped and thought it over. Orv Honeycutt had too valuable a horse to leave him tied there and sleep in the shed. It took a rash man to steal a horse in this country, but a Castañeda horse could make a man rash.

He groped his way carefully around the wagon yard, which was surrounded by a stout pole fence. In the corner farthest from both the wagon and the shed, a clump of short, bushy trees grew. He could hear a tied horse there, and in a moment could make it out, tearing at an armload of hay that had been thrown on the ground.

Then a match flared, lighting Honeycutt's haggard

face. When he had his cigarette going and spun the match away, it showed his shabby bedroll spread so that he could use his saddle for a pillow.

"Oh, lordie, lordie!" came his soft groan through the dark. His face was lighted redly as he pulled on the cigarette. "Oh, lordie, lordie," he said again.

Hewitt took hold of his .45 and twisted it to free the sight from the pawl that held it in his quick-draw holster. He edged to his right to take the horse out of his line of fire, and squatted down.

"Honeycutt, I've got you covered," he said. "Don't move and you'll be all right."

"Who is it?" Honeycutt quavered.

"Hewitt."

"Oh Jesus, Mr. Hewitt, what do you want with me?"

"You know what I want with you."

"Come on, let a fella alone, can't you? I ain't et since day before yestiddy. I'm sick, Mr. Hewitt. Real sick!"

"You'll be a damn sight sicker if you don't do as I say. Over on your hands and knees, now, facing me. Crawl this way and keep coming. I can blow a hole through you a yard across."

Honeycutt crawled toward him. Hewitt let him come within arm's reach.

"Sit up, but let's keep those hands in sight. There's no use waking the town up, but if you don't care, I sure as hell don't."

Honeycutt sat up. They could see each other now plainly. One thing that Hewitt saw was that Honeycutt was getting back his nerve. He was probably more afraid of George Boney than he was of Hewitt—and he had reason to be, having seen Boney beat three men's brains out.

"Mr. Hewitt," Honeycutt said, "there ain't no use of

you abusin' me, because I ain't done nothin' to you. That
damn George made me come along with him. I slipped
away from him yestiddy evenin', but I'm too sick to ride a
step."

"You lie."

"Mr. Hewitt, I swear to God—"

"Don't bother. Where is Boney now? When and where
do you meet him? Has he struck a deal with Domínguez,
or is Domínguez still having his fun with him? Those are
the things I'm interested in now. You don't have to tell
me anything about how you murdered Randall and Peeke
and Nicolas. I know all about that. I want to know now
how to get my hands on Boney."

He could see Honeycutt pulling his legs back to get his
knees under him. Hewitt was ready when he jumped. He
shifted the .45 to his left hand and snatched the limber-
necked, leather-covered, shot-filled sap from his hip
pocket.

He swung it once, giving it a snap of the wrist just before it connected. First it struck the brim of Honeycutt's
hat, but it caught Honeycutt in the middle of his forehead and dropped him inertly, his face in the mud.

Hewitt pocketed the sap, a weapon with which he was
an expert—a much-neglected one, too, he felt. With a
"cosh," as the fellows on the other side of the law usually
called them, you could disable a man without killing him
or even maiming him. If you knew how to use it, you
could do the same thing as a doctor did with chloroform,
only faster.

He pulled Honeycutt's bewhiskered face out of the
mud so that he could breathe and handcuffed his hands
behind him. He pulled him back into the deepest shadows under the trees and saddled the horse.

He returned to the shed, borrowed the lantern, and

hurried back to the street. There were still a few lonely
men about, but all the lights were out except for a few
nightlamps left burning in stores. He untied the restless
Coco and led him through the alley to the wagon lot. He
put the lantern down under the trees, put the bridle on
Honeycutt's horse, and stirred the man with his toe.

"Orv," he said softly. "Time to rise and shine."

Honeycutt was still unconscious. Hewitt picked him up
and heaved him across his own saddle. He removed the
handcuffs and put them in his pocket. He used Honeycutt's own rope to tie him, looping wrists to legs
under the horse's belly.

He walked, leading both horses, through the wagon
gate. A mosquito smudge-fire was smoking away beside
the one wagon in the lot. Beside it a family slept—man,
woman, and several small children. The man raised his
head and reached for his gun.

"Easy, there," Hewitt said softly. "Don't wake this sot
up, if you please. If he starts seeing snakes again, nobody
will sleep from here to Dallas."

"Oh," said the man. He put his gun down and turned
over to pull the blanket up over one of the children.

Hewitt was several miles out of town, heading east
through the willows and into the gulf swamps, when
Orval Honeycutt began moaning. Hewitt ignored him. In
a few moments the moaning changed to weeping.

It was still some time to daylight but the sky had lightened perceptibly, and Hewitt could see as well as hear
when Honeycutt began struggling. It took him a moment
to realize where he was. Hewitt let him suffer awhile,
until he had penetrated the willows so deeply that it was
unsafe to push further in the dark.

He stopped then and tied both horses to trees. He untied Honeycutt but did not offer to help him off the horse.

Honeycutt slid off, lost his balance, and sat down hard. The spirited horse humped himself out of the way, and Honeycutt yelled and scrambled in the other direction.

"Don't bother. I've got it," Hewitt said when he saw Honeycutt claw at his holster.

Honeycutt stumbled to his feet, rubbing his wrists where the rope had chafed them. He put a hand to his throbbing forehead and looked around in the gloom.

"Where the hell air we, Mr. Hewitt?" he asked piteously. "Where you takin' me?"

"Someplace where we can talk," said Hewitt.

"What about?"

"George Boney."

Honeycutt pressed his aching head harder. "Ain't no use you askin' about George. I'm a dead man if he gits after me."

"You're a dead man anyway, then."

Honeycutt shook his head stubbornly. "Boney ain't his real name, I kin tell you that much, but that's all," he said. "They's a reward out for him, a thousand dollars, dead or alive."

"Hell, Orv," Hewitt said, "there's already more than that on you for the three murders the other day. You don't think Don Aristide is going to let you get away with that, do you?"

Honeycutt looked down miserably at the ground. "I told you," he said, "George done that, and if I hadn't went with him, he'd've done me the same way. You don't have no idee what that man's like."

"What happened at Charco Verdugo? Tell me about the hanging of Mose Kirk—the truth this time."

Honeycutt gave a start at the sudden change of topic, but he shook his head and still did not look up. Hewitt looked about. There was now enough light to make out the dense willows clearly. They were well inland from the tide waters, but he had no doubt that this area occasionally was inundated by hurricane tides. Certainly it was not a place that would tempt casual visitors.

He took out his gun. "Start walking," he said, pointing with it.

"Come on, Mr. Hewitt, you cain't kill a man in cold blood," Honeycutt said.

"Can't I?" said Hewitt. "Walk!"

It was no pleasure to abuse any man, but there was a job to be done and to have the nerve to do it, Hewitt had only to think of the body dangling under the cottonwood at Charco Verdugo and the three dead ones near where they had crossed the Rio Grande. He drove Honeycutt ahead of him at gunpoint, deeper and deeper into the willows.

"You can stop now," he said at last.

Honeycutt stopped and looked around at Hewitt with a face as gray as a dead man's. Hewitt shifted the gun to his left hand again and took out the handcuffs. At a gesture, Honeycutt raised both wrists.

"You've done this before, haven't you?" Hewitt said, snapping one cuff around the right wrist. "Now put your arms around the tree there."

It was a willow eight inches thick, with long, trailing branches that seemed to shelter millions of mosquitoes. He had to jab Honeycutt sharply with the gun, but finally the man leaned against the tree and put his arms around it.

There, Hewitt snapped the other cuff. Almost before the prisoner realized it, his face was covered with mosquitoes. Hewitt blew a cloud of smoke at him and drove them off. He took another cigar from his pocket and stuck it in Honeycutt's mouth. He struck a match and held it for him.

"Draw, man, draw," he said. "But make it last. I'll try to get back here before it's all gone, but I can't promise. If I do make it back, I want the truth as fast as you can give it to me. Otherwise, you can stay here until somebody finds your bones."

"God damn it, Mr. Hewitt," Honeycutt said, "you cain't do this to a man."

"Can you tell me about hanging Mose Kirk, and those other three killings?"

Honeycutt closed his eyes and leaned against the tree, but he kept puffing the cigar. Hewitt walked away and left him there.

Forty minutes later, he was at the brick house where Conrad, Aristide, and his family were still sleeping. It was only twenty minutes after five, but as Hewitt turned Coco into the small corral and tied Honeycutt's horse to the fence, he could hear the rhythmic sound of cantering horses on the road.

Down the lane they came, Major Lafe Wisdom riding smartly in the lead, behind him a young lieutenant and a dozen hardbitten, capable-looking old troopers. Lafe recognized Hewitt and spurred ahead.

"What luck!" he shouted. "Todd's in Matamoros. Only had a minute to talk to him, but he said if they's anything like General Domínguez's new mounts, he'll go as high as a hundred and fifty apiece."

He swung out of the saddle to stand beside Hewitt. The troopers pulled up a respectful distance away. Hewitt pointed at the horse he had taken from Honeycutt.

"How do you like that fellow, Lafe?" he said. "Five years old, and look at that chest—look at those legs and feet! I've seen him go for over a week, and he'll wear you out and keep going."

"Almost as pretty as your horse," Lafe said. "Who does he belong to?"

"You. Not as a commission, because we haven't got a deal and I don't think we're going to have one. I'm selling you that horse with a bill of sale signed by the owner for one dollar."

"Why won't we have a deal?"

"Your friend Todd must think he's dealing with a greenhorn. Fifty-seven hundred is cheap for these horses. Come look at them. Bring your men."

He walked them to the back corral, where José's men stood guard over the herd. Hewitt told José to run the carriage teams into a separate corral. Conrad came out of the pergola, wearing his derby and tying his necktie, to join them.

"Lafe, my friend and partner, Conrad Meuse," Hewitt said. "Conrad, Major Lafe Wisdom. We worked together on the Stoneman case."

"I remember hearing the name," Conrad said. "How do you do, Major. We have met on the street, I'm sure."

"Yes, nice to know any friend of Jeff's," Wisdom said nervously. He looked around at Hewitt after they had shaken hands. "I count thirty-four head there, Jeff. God, man, at a hundred and fifty apiece, that's fifty-one hundred dollars! You can't let a measly six hundred dollars stand in the way of a fast deal."

"Wrong," Hewitt said. "I can, and it's a good bit more than six hundred dollars, Lafe."

Conrad, with a straight face, muttered something in German: "Let us see how you negotiate a deal, my friend." Hewitt nodded and smiled at him.

"The fifty-seven hundred," he said to Wisdom, "is for

thirty-two horses, deal closed at six o'clock. The two other horses are two hundred each—at six o'clock. That's a total of sixty-one hundred—at six o'clock. At seven o'clock, the price goes up to sixty-two hundred. At eight, I make my own deal with General Domínguez."

A moment of silence. "Lieutenant, wait here for me," Wisdom said. "By God, Jeff, you're a hard man in a horse trade, I'll say that for you. I'll go see Todd now."

"I'll ride part of the way with you."

"Todd wants these horses for the officer corps. In fact, he's over there trying to buy some from the general for his list."

"It's up to him," Hewitt said indifferently. "The general isn't selling, Lafe. He's buying—if he can."

They rode together until they neared town. Lafe kept on toward the international bridge. Hewitt doubled back and, making sure no one was following him, turned Coco into the willows. He quickly found the tracks he had made earlier, and was relieved to see that there were no others.

He dismounted and tied Coco. The stallion was tired, hungry, and in a bad temper, and the mosquitoes drove him crazy. Hewitt walked to where he had left Honeycutt handcuffed to the tree. He could have felt sorry for him, had he not been seeing Mose Kirk's body so clearly in his mind.

The cigar had not lasted long. Honeycutt's face was so badly swollen from mosquito bites that his eyes were almost closed. Hewitt unlocked the handcuffs and told him to start walking. The man stumbled only a few steps before he fell down.

Hewitt picked him up and carried him to where he could put him in Coco's saddle. He locked the handcuffs on his wrists and began leading the horse out of the willows.

There were several little houses occupied by Mexican families near the edge of Brownsville. Hewitt stopped there and asked an old woman for water for his prisoner. She brought a pail fresh from the well, and a gourd dipper. Hewitt handed it up to Honeycutt, who had to make a real effort to hold it to drink.

He drank the gourd dry. Hewitt refilled it. Honeycutt emptied it again. "Mr. Hewitt," he said, "I'm so hungry, I'm like to faint."

"You'll be fed whenever you're ready to talk."

"I'm a dead man if I do."

"You're a dead man if you don't."

"Where air you takin' me?"

"I'm turning you over to the sheriff—as soon as I'm through with you. Orv, you're going to do some time in prison on those murders. The more you talk, the less time you'll do. That's the way it works, and you know it."

"I cain't do no time if I'm dead, Mr. Hewitt. You just don't know that son of a bitch of a Boney!"

"Suit yourself." Hewitt turned to the Mexican woman and asked her, in Spanish, if she could feed his prisoner. It was clear that her sympathies were always with the underdog, but she nodded sullenly. "Orv," he went on, "you can eat right now if you're ready to do business. The safest place for you then is jail."

"I'll talk," Honeycutt said.

CHAPTER FIFTEEN

Honeycutt's story, mumbled through swollen lips as he
munched fried beans and sipped tripe soup, brought back
vividly the scene at Charco Verdugo. It was almost—
almost—like the story George Boney himself had told.
There was the same overbearing colonel commanding the
same smart troops, and the same greedy bullying over
who owned the fine horses.

But there were differences.

"Listen here," Boney told Honeycutt, Peeke, and Randall, the moment the soldiers came into sight, "these goddamn horses is done fer. You fellers hold them and let me
make the best deal I can make, and we'll take it and
cut for the river."

He was their leader, their commander, their boss,
wasn't he? They were already in trouble over firing at the
rurales, weren't they? They were still a long, hard ride
from the border, weren't they? Tired, hungry, with a herd
of wild horses on their hands, what the hell help were
they getting from Don Aristide and Hewitt and the Mexican guards?

Honeycutt, Randall, and Peeke did their best to hold
the horses at the waterhole while Boney rode out to meet
the soldiers. Something went wrong from the beginning.

Something Boney said infuriated Domínguez, who slapped Boney across the mouth twice with his heavy gloves. The colonel had two of his men disarm Boney and put a rope on him.

But Boney was still putting up an argument when they came within hearing distance. "I told you, these horses has already been sold by an American to the Mexican Army," Honeycutt heard him say. "They're expectin' us in Matamoros tomorrow, the general himself. If we don't turn up, all hell's gonna break loose."

"What general? What's his name?" Domínguez said with a skeptical smile.

"How do I know? Whoever is commandin'."

"What American owns these horses?"

"His name," Boney said, "is Jefferson Hewitt, and he's a big, rich politician and a friend of President Díaz."

"I think these horses belong to Castañeda."

"They did once. They belong to Hewitt now."

"Castañeda is nobody, nobody! The President will wipe him out."

"Mebbe that's why he sold the horses to Mr. Hewitt. Look here, you give us a thousand dollars apiece and we'll hit fer the border and never stop ridin' until we's closer to Canada than we are Mexico."

"It would be cheaper to shoot you, my friend."

"You'll think so, mebbe, until that general in Matamoros sees who has his horses. Mister, you need a bill of sale, and I kin write one out and sign it fer you," Boney said.

He saw the colonel hesitating, and went on, "I turn the bill of sale over to you now, but me and my men deliver the horses to you in Reynosa. You don't pay us nothin' until we git there. A thousand apiece—why, this herd is worth three times that!"

He almost had Colonel Domínguez convinced—only just then Mose Kirk rode in.

Colonel Domínguez read the note Hewitt had written, relieving Boney and putting Mose in charge. He knew how narrowly he had escaped being made a fool, but he still needed Boney. He was on a military mission and would be late enough getting back to Reynosa. If he came in with a herd of fine, strange horses, he might come out of it a hero. But he still had some explaining to do to his own superiors.

He needed Boney even more after he had ordered Kirk hanged. The colonel had lived too long on the border not to know how hard President Díaz was trying to stabilize relations with the United States and pacify the border.

He was able to raise a hundred twenty dollars in American money among his officers. He had Boney write him out a bill of sale for the horses. He gave him the money and a receipt showing that he had "appropriated" the horses in the name of his government. He was then protected—as far as ownership of the horses went.

But he still had hanged an American and he was running late on his mission. He detailed one troop to start the horses toward Reynosa. "We will take your own horses—saddles and all—and put you afoot as though we had robbed you. Your own people will rescue you, and you will have a good story to tell about losing the horses," he told Boney.

"No!" Boney shouted. "I won't stand fer it. I don't like it one damn bit."

The colonel jerked his thumb toward Mose Kirk, whose body was twirling slowly in the breeze at the end of a braided leather rope. "Would you like that better? That is your only choice," he said.

Two minutes later, he was off to the southwest with the

rest of his command. Boney skimmed twenty dollars off the top of the hundred twenty in cash and divided the balance four ways. They then mounted up, only to be put afoot a few miles from the charco.

What still seemed to grieve Honeycutt more than anything else was the fact that Boney had come out of it with forty-five dollars while the others got only twenty-five dollars each. Still worse, he was sure that Boney had robbed the bodies of Peeke and Randall after killing them, and kept that money, too.

Honeycutt was a broken man, and the food only robbed him of the last of his strength to resist. "You know what his real name is, Mr. Hewitt?" he said. "He told me himself, to skeer me."

"Did it?"

Honeycutt shivered. "You damn betcha it did! You ever hear of a feller by the name of Jim Barkalow, that's wanted in Kansas?"

"Yes. Shot a man in the back, stole his wife, abused her, and then killed her."

"And killed a deputy sheriff that went after him. Mr. Hewitt, he *bragged* about that to me! He bragged they's a thousand-dollars reward for him dead or alive!"

"We'll clear that one up, then, won't we?"

"Reckon so. Seems to me I'd be entitled to part of that reward, Mr. Hewitt."

"I doubt that, Orv. And I'm more interested in the death of Mose Kirk."

"Why, that wasn't no American crime," Honeycutt said wonderingly. "That happened in Mexico. Cain't no American court try nobody for that. Besides, that fool kid, he brung it on himself. He'd still be alive today if he'd had one goddamn lick of sense."

"Would he?"

"How do you mean that, Mr. Hewitt?"

"Dugan Peeke and Blackie Randall aren't alive, are they? And you're just barely. Orv, it's a good thing for you I made my deal to turn you over to the sheriff before you and I had this little talk. It would be a pleasure to hang you higher than Haman, personally."

"Who was Haman?"

"You two would have hit it off just fine. Come on, let's go."

He handcuffed Honeycutt again and let him ride a quarter of a mile. He made him dismount, then, and walk ahead of him into town. He held Coco down to a stately, curveting walk and let all the townspeople get a good look at him bringing in his prisoner. He had long ago learned that, in dealing with local policemen, it was well to make certain things clear from the beginning.

"I seem to recognize these handcuffs," the sheriff said when Hewitt turned the prisoner over to him.

"Yes," said Hewitt. "Major Wisdom borrowed them last night—I believe from one of your deputies."

The sheriff was serving his first term and was not yet sure of himself. He was no more than forty, a lean, silent, suspicious man who probably was just as tough as he thought he was.

"If you knowed they was a prisoner to be took in," he said, "I don't see why you didn't tell my man and let us do it. I don't take kindly to a private detective butting into my affairs."

"There wasn't time, sheriff." Hewitt was bone tired, but he put on his most winning smile. "Your name is Stern, isn't it?"

"Bill Stern, that's right."

"I imagine we're going to hear quite a bit more of Bill Stern in the future. I see a lot of sheriffs, Bill, and I'm an old hand at this business. You're going to be one of the good ones, and you've got a tough county to police. Major Wisdom speaks highly of you."

"He does?"

"Yes, indeed. What I'd like to do now, Bill, is eat about a week's supply of breakfast somewhere, and have somebody notify me the minute Major Wisdom shows up on the street. I want to see him and he wants to see me."

"Well, I'll tell you, Mr. Hewitt—"

"Jeff's the name, Bill."

"Yes, you bet. The Lone Star is the best bet if it's good, filling grub you want, and I'll see to it you know about the major. Pleasure to help you, Jeff."

Hewitt had barely started to eat when Wisdom came striding into the saloon, beating his hat against his leg. "God damn," he said, "it's starting to rain again. Six thousand, Todd says."

"Who gets the horses from him?"

"The officer corps of the good old U.S.A. cavalry. He's waiting to hear."

"Where?"

"Over to his shipping pens."

"Not in Matamoros?"

Wisdom said impatiently, "How about it, will you sell? Jeff, I'm so dead set on owning that horse, I'm like a kid on Christmas Eve. And I can't take it and let my fellow officers down—you know that!"

Hewitt stopped eating. "Do you know what kind of mood General Domínguez is in?"

"I know he blistered Todd's hide off, but, man, six thousand dollars is waiting for you to say 'yes.' Can't this wait?"

"Can you bring Mr. Todd here?" Hewitt asked. "I'm

going to make a deal with him, but not unless and until he can help me a little, too."

"Back in five minutes, Jeff." Wisdom turned to hurry out. He had taken no more than six steps when he stopped and whirled. "By the way, Jeff," he said, dropping his voice, "that picture you've got—I saw that chap in Matamoros. He was talking to Todd, in fact."

Hewitt hoped he did not betray the excitement he felt. "Lafe," he said, "will Todd want to see the horses first? That would seem to make more sense to me."

"I'll see. He'll take my word on a horse, I think, but yes, he should look at them himself."

"I'll wait here exactly forty minutes."

Wisdom merely nodded and hurried out.

CHAPTER SIXTEEN

"They are beautiful horses," said J. Grover Todd, "but there's something queer going on here, Mr. Hewitt, if you don't mind my saying so."

"I don't," said Hewitt. "May I pour you another drink, while I tell you what I think it is?"

"One more," Todd said, suspiciously.

"You too, Lafe?"

"A short one. You know me, Jeff, when there's a horse up for takin's. I'd sell my soul, that I would."

J. Grover Todd was a native of New York City, a cultivated man who had lost one fortune speculating on horses. He loved them as much as ever, but he had become a sternly self-disciplined dealer now. He raised his glass and sipped the whiskey, watching Hewitt with slitted gray eyes.

"General Domínguez," Hewitt said, "wouldn't sell, I'm sure."

"Go on, you're telling this."

"Flew into a rage, I imagine, when he heard that there were more horses of the same blood and build for sale here."

"That's what puzzles me, Mr. Hewitt. They're so obvi-

ously the same stock, the same breeder had to have bred
them."

"He did indeed. You'll meet him, he'll sign your bill of
sale, he'll tell you about his Kentucky and Irish and
French studs. I wonder what your impression of the general is, though, outside of horses."

Todd's eyes narrowed still more. "In what way? What
difference does it make?"

"Suppose you were President Díaz—how safe would
you feel with this fellow commanding at Matamoros?"

Todd seemed to make up his mind. "I met Porfirio Díaz
years ago. He wouldn't remember me, but let's put it this
way—I only wish I knew some way to warn him about
this jaybird. Domínguez is a headstrong fool. He has lost
the support of his officers—even I could tell that—and I
think he's for sale."

"Who promoted him to general officer, do you know?"

"I do not. My feeling is that he promoted himself. He
commands the best mounted troops east of Chihuahua. I
don't know who is going to *de*mote him so long as he has
those men behind him."

Hewitt nodded. "What do you think of President Díaz?
I'm not asking idly, Mr. Todd. All this has an important
purpose."

"I knew Benito Juárez. I admired him very much. I did
not think much of Díaz for turning against him and I was
glad when he lost. But Juárez is dead. There is a hole in
the bucket that only Porfirio Díaz can plug." Todd
pounded the table softly with his fist. "I agree with our
own Secretary of State—Mexico lives or dies with Díaz
today. Later—who knows about any politician? But we're
talking about today."

"Do you happen to know a young captain by the name
of Gilberto Martínez?"

"Afraid not."

"Too bad." Hewitt took the picture of George Boney from his pocket. "Is this fellow familiar?"

"That degenerate, impudent bastard!" Todd said after only a glance at the picture. "He had the presumption to tell me that the horses Domínguez has actually belong to him. He offered me one third of them to take him in to where he could assassinate Domínguez. The man's a lunatic, Mr. Hewitt."

"His real name," said Hewitt, "is James Barkalow, and he's wanted in Kansas for a vicious double murder. Where did you last see him?"

"Skulking in a cantina just across the river, la Casa de la Luna Pálida it's called. It's one of the places American soldiers are forbidden to enter. You know the type."

Hewitt nodded. He leaned back and let his tired mind sift the conflicting factors of the problems he faced. It was like juggling eggs. Todd waited with the patience of a born horse trader, but Lafe Wisdom was impatient.

"Mr. Todd," Hewitt said at last, "I want you to go with me to see the gentleman who owns these horses. I want to get a bill of sale somewhere and fill it out so he can sign it personally."

"I carry them in my saddlebags," Todd said.

"Fine, but we may have a problem with Señor Castañeda. He's a rich man, but he's a refugee from Mexico by choice. On the kind of whim that only a rich man can afford, he has declared against President Díaz."

"Then he's a fool."

Hewitt nodded. "I don't quite know how he's going to react to that fellow Domínguez strutting about with a general's epaulettes on a Castañeda horse. I'll have to rely on inspiration, and I hope you will support me."

"Anything to close this deal. I have other things to do."

"Then let's make out the bill of sale and have it ready for him to sign, and hope for the best."

All the way out to Aristide's place, Todd studied Coco surreptitiously and the big stallion showed off as though he knew he was under observation. Todd's fine gray gelding was worth a lot of money, but he was not half the horse Coco was. Todd was too good a horse trader to give himself away, yet he was also too good a horseman not to want Coco more with every moment that passed.

Which could be still another complication. Hewitt needed Todd's help now, but the man was a fanatic about horses. Nothing else would count if he saw a chance to get Coco.

Conrad Meuse and the women were sitting in the pergola. It was again threatening rain, and the humidity had become intense. Josefina got up and hurried into the house as they dismounted and tied near the side door. Helen looked after her with a worried expression, shaking her head. She murmured something to Conrad, who came to meet them.

Wisdom was staring out past the pergola to where the cavalrymen lounged in the shade, and beyond them to the horses. The one that Honeycutt had ridden, that was to be his, had been tied under a tree. Lafe stared at him with the same fanatical yearning that Todd felt—and he was not horse trader enough to hide it.

Hewitt introduced Conrad and Todd. "I've sold the horses to Mr. Todd," he said, "and we need Aristide's signature on the bill of sale."

Conrad looked troubled. "It would be too bad to bother him now. He has many worries."

Josefina being most of them, no doubt. Hewitt felt sorry for Aristide, and even sorrier for the girl, but there was no way out. Events were pressing him, with a recklessly am-

bitious adventurer commanding all the troops in Matamoros and a homicidal maniac plotting to assassinate
him.

"It can't be helped," Hewitt said. "I've got to see him
and I've got to bear down on him. I know what I'm doing
and you're going to have to support me on it."

"You give me no choice."

No, Hewitt thought as he led the way into the house,
and you'll make me sweat for it someday. . . . Aristide
was not in the hot little living room, but they could hear
his voice coming from the kitchen, and Josefina's. They
were speaking in French, to keep the servants out of it.
Aristide was pleading with Josefina not to be rash about
something.

Hewitt called his name. Aristide came in, looking ten
years older than he had last night. It came to Hewitt suddenly what was wrong here, why Josefina had hurried
into the house, why Helen looked so worried, why Aristide looked to be at the end of his rope. Probably Josefina
had confirmed that she was carrying Mose Kirk's child.

Again Hewitt introduced Todd. "I've sold him the
horses," he said, "and we need your signature on a bill of
sale. It's all prepared."

Aristide looked at Conrad and then back at Hewitt.
"Very well, if you feel it that important," he said. "I am
still more concerned about that other matter."

"I told you, I'll take care of that later." Aristide meant,
of course, the diamonds, but Hewitt felt fairly 'sure that
the diamonds really did not matter that much today. Aristide's bitterness was so deep, and his need for a scapegoat
so great, that nothing would please him today.

"Later, later, always later," Aristide said. "I had
counted on you for more than words, friend Hewitt, but
very well, let us have the bill of sale."

Todd handed it over. Aristide merely glanced at it and handed it to Conrad, who read it rapidly and handed it back. Aristide brought ink and a steel pen from another room and sat down at a small table to sign his elaborate signature.

Hewitt nodded to Todd and Wisdom to sit down, too. "There is one other thing, Aristide," he said.

Aristide was blowing on the signature to dry the ink. "Is it important?"

"Yes. That fellow that took your horses, Domínguez, has promoted himself to general's rank. He's now commanding across the river, with the best regular troops in northern Mexico."

"On my horses."

"Yes."

"You gave young Martínez my horses, too."

"I did indeed, and it may have been the smartest thing I ever did. Now it's time for you to put aside your prejudices and do the smart as well as the handsome and honorable thing, Aristide."

Aristide raised his eyebrows. "Oh?"

Confidence came to Hewitt in a surge as he saw the pain and bewilderment in Aristide's eyes. There were times when you split your openers to draw four and you knew that nothing on earth could stop the right four from falling.

"Martínez," he said, "will not go far from Charco Verdugo until he has whipped his command into shape. I want to get a message to him, and I want you to sign it."

"Indeed? And what will this message say?"

"That he is to remain close to Reynosa—certainly no farther than Charco Verdugo—to await important orders from President Díaz."

Aristide stared at him. "*Ai Dios,* is that all you expect of me?"

"No. I want you to send a telegram to the President, telling him you have changed your mind and are coming to his support. No, God damn it," Hewitt said, raising his voice as Aristide leaped to his feet, "you listen to me! You have already lost your horses. You're not going to get them back. It's time to do the handsome thing and give them to your government freely."

"You make it impossible to be civil to you," Aristide shouted. "That man is an intriguer, a usurper, a bandit—"

"He is the President of Mexico," Hewitt cut in, "and either you're a patriot or you're not—either you're a Mexican or you're a shabby outcast who declines to share the suffering of his own people. Damn the horses, Aristide! They're only a token. You offer them to Díaz, yes, but only as a symbol of the loyalty you wish to express to the legally elected President of your own country.

"Damn it, man, can't you see what's going to happen if Díaz loses support and is replaced by still another *Presidente proclamado?* Do you want French and British gunboats occupying your ports and collecting your tariffs to pay the interest on Mexican bonds that they hold? Do you want another Austrian emperor, perhaps, supported by another European army commanded by another Bazaine?

"Aristide, when Zaragosa whipped the French at Puebla, Porfirio Díaz was a young officer in the Army of Juárez. You were a schoolboy in England then. Díaz has credentials that no rich émigré can challenge. A man in your position has a very narrow choice. Either you're a Mexican or you're an enemy of Mexico. Which are you?"

Suddenly J. Grover Todd spoke up—in French, one cultivated man to another. "He's right, you know. It is time for all Mexicans to stand together, and your example would have enormous effect. As the North goes, so goes Mexico. I speak as one who observes from the outside, and I tell you, this man Domínguez is dangerous to President Díaz and to your country."

Aristide collected his wits and his dignity. "I would find it difficult," he said, in French, "to offer my support to Díaz, but it could be done. But I do not see what the hurry is, and I do not understand why I must also send a message to Gilberto Martínez—I do not even see what young Martínez has to do with it."

Todd switched to English. "Neither do I. I don't even know this Martínez."

"He is a good man, the son of an old, old friend."

"He's a captain in the volunteers," said Hewitt, "and the logical man to succeed Domínguez in command at Matamoros."

"From captain to general?" Aristide cried. "And he is so young, so inexperienced!"

"Domínguez went from colonel to general overnight," said Hewitt, "and at least Martínez is nearby."

"But if Domínguez is as you say, do you really feel he would turn over command to anyone?"

Todd's eyes met Hewitt's briefly. "Señor Castañeda," Todd said, "let me put it this way—I have a fairly strong conviction that Domínguez will be turning over command to someone soon—why not your friend?"

Aristide looked at Hewitt. "Very well, I suppose it is what I have wanted to do all along. But the wires are not open on the coast. How is a telegram to go?"

"By way of El Paso," said Hewitt, "and if you mark it 'urgent, diplomatic service,' it will be on its way from El Paso in an hour."

"But I am not in the diplomatic service."

"Nobody knows that in the telegraph company. It will be in Mexico City before anyone figures out what to do. I live by the telegraph. I know! The telegrapher can either send a wire or refuse to send it, and it's always easier to send it than to argue."

"Write what you want me to say to the President, then, and I'll sign it."

Hewitt took note that Aristide had referred to Díaz as "the President," the first time he had ever heard him use that title. "I'll write it in English," he said. "You put.it into Spanish."

"Make it sonorous, like organ music," Aristide said. "Porfirio must be in tears before he comes to my name at the end, you understand?"

Hewitt sat down at the table. Aristide went for paper. Major Wisdom could stand it no longer.

"Mr. Todd, you won't need my men to help with those horses now, will you?"

"No, Major, thank you very much."

"I'll be off, then. I have things to do," Wisdom said eagerly.

He almost ran from the room. A few moments later, Hewitt heard the detail passing the house. Through the front window, he got a glimpse of the soldiers. Wisdom had put his McClellan saddle on the Honeycutt horse, and rode him as proudly as if he were one of Napoleon's marshals. The only trouble was, he had forgotten all about getting a bill of sale for him.

Thirty minutes later, Hewitt, Todd, and José were on their way into Brownsville. José would turn back to the ford where they had crossed the river, and head south to Charco Verdugo with Aristide's letter to Captain Martínez. Todd carried the bill of sale for Wisdom's horse as well as the one for his own horses.

Hewitt carried the precious telegram that was to be dispatched with the "urgent—diplomatic" flag. The moment they reached the public road, Todd said abruptly, "Mr. Hewitt, how much do you want for that horse?"

"See me tomorrow, Mr. Todd," Hewitt said.

Todd nodded as though he understood.

CHAPTER SEVENTEEN

Two things Hewitt badly needed—sleep and information, in that order. He could go a long time without rest, and then sleep a long time catching up, but he had already reached his limit and he knew it. He knew what he wanted to do but he did not feel sharp and decisive about it.

He was sure that George Boney—or Jim Barkalow, as he was known in Kansas—would not show himself on the American side of the line. There was a kid Hewitt had used before, a boy of American citizenship but Mexican parentage. He had always hung around the border crossing, picking up a dollar here and a peso there. He could learn more in an hour or two than most detectives could in that many days.

Benito was his name. Although Hewitt walked the muddy street for several minutes, leading Coco almost to the international bridge, he saw no sign of the boy. It did not surprise him. The best of kids could come to a bad end in this hell-hole, and if the spectacular stallion did not attract Benito's attention, he simply was not there.

He would have to throw himself on Sheriff Bill Stern's mercy. He mounted Coco and rode to the sheriff's office in a corner of the old military compound once known as

Fort Brown. The sheriff was alone, bringing his official accounts up to date.

"What's up, Jeff?" he said cordially. "What can I do for you? Want to see your prisoner?"

"No, Bill, thanks," Hewitt said. He took the chair that Stern indicated. "I've got to catch a little sleep, and I wish that meanwhile I had a connection in Matamoros that could pick up some information for me. If you know somebody there, that might help."

Stern shook his head regretfully. "Did have, but this new commanding general, Domínguez, is firing people right and left. It amounts to martial law, Jeff, and I don't like it worth a damn. You know what I'm afraid of?"

"I think I can guess. He'll start trouble with the United States, to force Díaz to back him. Otherwise, he might be relieved, and he damn well knows it."

"That's it."

You had to make quick decisions, sometimes, on taking people into your confidence. "That's part of my problem, Bill," Hewitt said. "This must be strictly between you and me, but I think that fellow's hand is going to be forced soon, perhaps today, certainly no later than tomorrow. That's why I need to know what's going on over there, so I'll know what cards I hold when I've caught forty winks."

Stern's face lengthened. "The one thing I can't do—or let you do—is mix in Mexican politics."

"I won't be mixing in it. My client is a wealthy Mexican, a friend of Porfirio Díaz." At least, Hewitt thought, I can hope he is or will be soon. . . . "But there are reasons I can't show my face there personally, yet."

Stern was gloomily silent for a moment. Any sheriff here would be sitting on a lid that covered a long history of violence. The American flag had first been raised here in 1846, and the last battle of the Civil War had been fought near here almost a month after Lee's surrender. Stern's constituency had more voters of Mexican descent than of American.

Across the river lay as tough a town as any in the world. Matamoros was a critical cornerstone in any Mexican administration, yet it was far from the capital. Now it was being run by a strutting outlaw in a soldier's uniform—and the hell of it was, he commanded the best troops, some of them now mounted on the best horses, in the entire northern part of Mexico.

Mexicans still had not forgiven the United States for the territory it had lost after the war between the two nations. The beloved Benito Juárez had been able to take refuge in the United States, after his defeat by French troops supporting Emperor Maximilian. Juárez had made friendship with the United States a key part of his program. Díaz was friendly, too.

But if Domínguez started trouble with the Americans, if he waved the bloody shirt, shot a few cool heads, shouted the old slogans, and promised enough loot to *voluntarios*, Díaz could be in real trouble, with another revolution on his hands.

"Sir, Major Wisdom claims you're a man of judgment," Stern said suddenly, "and God knows there's little of that around. Tell you what, I've got a feller here that sweeps out for me and takes care of my horses and garden, while he goes to school. He gen'ly can find out what's going on over there."

He got up, slouched to the door leading to the jail cells, and said in Spanish, "Come here for a minute, boy. I want you to talk to a friend of mine."

A wiry lad who looked to be about fourteen or fifteen came into the room. His eyes betrayed his pleasure at seeing Hewitt, but otherwise he showed no emotion. "If this gringo is a friend of yours, Bill," he said in perfect English, "I would rather talk to your enemies."

Hewitt shot to his feet and put out his hand. "Benito, you scoundrel, you've gotten respectable," he said.

"Only on the surface, Mr. Hewitt, only on the surface," Benito said, flushing with pleasure as he shook hands.

"I see you two know each other," said Stern. "This whelp is my brother-in-law, Jeff. Marry a Mexican girl and you've married her whole family, you know."

Suddenly there was no constraint between them. They sat down with their heads close together, talking in low voices. Hewitt had to take them into his confidence completely. The boy, Benito, was going to have to scout Matamoros. He could not send the kid over there ignorant of the dangerous possibilities.

"I've got to get some sleep, Benito," he said, "and if we have any luck, by the time I wake up, General Domínguez should have had a telegram from President Díaz, relieving him of command."

"He won't pay any attention to it," Benito said. "I tell you, Mr. Hewitt, he's just crazy enough to want to be President himself."

"He'll have to do something. It will at least force his hand. If our luck holds, a good man will be promoted to general's rank to succeed him, a fellow by the name of Gilberto Martínez, from somewhere around Ciudad Victoria."

"I know him," said Benito. "He's a good man, but he's only a captain of volunteers. How could he be promoted to general?"

"You let me worry about that. I don't *know* that it's going to happen, but that's where my money is."

Benito frowned. "Domínguez will never turn over command to anyone. This regiment is the old *Lanceros*. It fought at Buena Vista. It rode right over the American artillery there. It has fought the French, the *Yanquis*. I have seen its captured battle flags."

Hewitt let him talk it out. Benito might be an American, but he had been named for the great Juárez, and he took immense pride in his Mexican heritage.

"It is too bad," Benito went on, "that it is under such a man as Domínguez. If only Martínez could command it! But I tell you, Mr. Hewitt, this loco will never give it up—never!"

"We'll see," Hewitt said. "If everything goes right, Domínguez should get the bad news this afternoon sometime. I want to know what he does."

"He'll parade his troops, that's what he'll do," said Benito. "He'll gallop them through Matamoros to show his power, and form them up somewhere near the river where the Americans can see. What good is a telegram when you command *los Lanceros?*"

"You're probably right, Benito, but that's the kind of thing I have to know. While you're waiting for it to happen, there's a man, an American, hiding out in the Casa de la Luna Pálida. Know what that is?"

"Yes," said Benito, "and do you know what those pale moons are? You can get something from those girls that you can bring back without paying duty."

Hewitt grinned. He unrolled the picture that he and Aristide had drawn of Boney. "This is the man," he said, "and he won't be thinking about girls. He may be doing some drinking, but not enough to put him under. Now, here comes the tricky part, Benito, so please pay very careful attention."

Benito nodded. Sheriff Stern scowled. "Yes, sir," Benito said. "I can see how it could be very tricky, Mr. Hewitt.

This is the man who has been trying to make General Domínguez pay him ten thousand dollars."

Stern started. He leaned back in his chair and rammed his hands into his pockets. "What the hell's going on here, Jeff?" he said.

"If you don't know, Bill," said Hewitt, "you can't be blamed for anything, can you?"

"Now, by God, I told you there was to be no interference in Mexican politics!"

"Tell that to George Boney."

"This man?" Stern tapped the picture. "What do you reckon he means to do?"

"Nothing that you can prevent, with him on one side of the border and you on the other. Nothing I want to prevent."

"What the hell *do* you want?"

"I want," Hewitt said, "for Benito to skin back here the minute he has reason to believe that Domínguez has received a telegram. I want to know what Domínguez is going to do. But on his way back, I want Benito to stop in la Casa de la Luna Pálida and drop the word to this gringo what Domínguez is going to do, too."

"Man," Stern burst out, "do you realize what you may be starting?"

"I'm not starting anything," said Hewitt, "nor are you. Neither can you stop anything. Do you want to go over there and tell Domínguez that he's going to be relieved of his command—that there's an American drinking himself into a fit of fury in a cheap whorehouse—that *you* know what the President of Mexico is going to do before he does it? Do you call *that* not interfering in Mexican politics?"

Stern tried to roll a cigarette, but he was so agitated

that he ripped the paper. Hewitt handed him a cigar and
then held a match for him.

"I'll tell you this, Jeff," Stern said, between puffs, "this
Boney or whatever his name is don't know what he's get-
ting into, if he thinks he can get close enough to
Domínguez to kill him with a six-gun."

"That," said Hewitt, "is what worries me."

"I think it was in March," Benito said gently, "that that
fellow, the Englishman, reported that his Winchester was
stolen, wasn't it?"

"Yes, and it served him right, but—"

"I was in la Casa de la Luna Pálida only last week, and
there was a rifle on the wall in the back room. I *think* it
was a Winchester, a model seventy. But I am not sure,
and the Englishman is already gone, and how would you
get it back and send it to him if it was his?"

Stern stood up and clamped his big hat on his head.
"You're right, you're right, I don't want to know anything
about any of this, Jeff. Benito will take you to my place to
catch some sleep. I think I better get out to San Benito
and serve them papers. If anybody asks where I've went,
Benito, you tell them San Benito, you hear?"

Hewitt and Benito walked to Stern's house, leading
Coco. The boy was eager to get across the river, where
the excitement would be if it came at all. He cautioned
Hewitt not to say anything about it to his sister, Stern's
wife.

"I won't," Hewitt said, "but you use your head, and
don't take any chances."

"I won't. I'm not crazy."

"What do you plan to make of yourself, Benito? You're
not going to sweep the office and take care of the sheriff's
horse all your life, are you?"

"No. I am going to be a lawyer. I am going to become

a rich lawyer and marry a beautiful wife with much money, and own twenty horses like this one."

"There aren't twenty like this one in the entire world, Benito."

"Then I shall have to have this one, and breed the ones I want from him."

Stern's wife was a poised and pretty woman, as intelligent as her brother. She gave Hewitt a Mexican snack, but she had American white bread in the oven and promised him fresh bread, ham and eggs, and strong coffee when he woke up.

CHAPTER EIGHTEEN

He came awake to the sound of thunder crashing overhead. His watch showed that it was a little past five. He dressed and checked his guns—the .45 he wore in the holster on his belly and the .38 in the shoulder holster.

Mrs. Stern heard him moving about and had his ham and eggs ready when he came out. The rain started as he sat down to eat. It was so dark in the house that Mrs. Stern lighted a lamp, but the blinding, blinking glare of lightning at times made it as bright as noon.

The storm was directly overhead. It would ease up eventually, but meanwhile it could change everything. No, Mrs. Stern said, Benito had not been there. But Stern had stopped in briefly, to say that the Mexican cavalry had mounted up and was parading at the gallop through Matamoros, making a racket audible all the way across the international bridge.

Before going on about his business elsewhere, Stern had left a black oilskin slicker for Hewitt to use. He was keeping hands off a very touchy situation—which was exactly what Hewitt wanted him to do.

It was still raining hard when Hewitt finished eating. He put on the slicker, which had been made for a taller man, and went out to saddle Coco. The horse had rested and eaten and wanted to run. Hewitt held him to a walk.

The military police were out in full force in Brownsville, some mounted and some afoot, and the horse-drawn ambulance used as a patrol wagon was tied in front of the Lone Star. There was no other horse at the hitchrail, and when Hewitt dismounted there, a soldier came out of the shelter of the roof that covered the plank sidewalk. He looked Coco over carefully.

"I wonder, sir," he said, "if you're Mr. Hewitt?"

"Yes, I am."

"Fine, then. Major Wisdom is inside. He'd like to see you, sir."

"Thank you, soldier. The town's pretty empty, it seems to me."

"Yes, sir. We're asking people not to tie at the saloons, and to stay off the streets."

He had said all he meant to say. Hewitt went into the Lone Star. Wisdom sat at the corner table with a captain and two sergeants.

"There you are," he said. "Damned if you haven't taken your time. Sit down, Jeff."

He introduced the men with him. Hewitt shook hands with them before sitting down. "The curtain," he said, "is about to go up, don't you think?"

"Some son of a bitch has been firing across the river with a rifle. Sergeant Herlihy, here, took a detail to the bridge to report it to the authorities, but there were no authorities. There's nobody guarding the bridge on their side."

"Those shots," said Hewitt, "could they have come from la Casa de la Luna Pálida?"

"They could have. I couldn't prove it. People who heard it say it wasn't a Mauser."

"They've got a Winchester model seventy there, from

what I hear. If Boney could pick off an American soldier or two with it, he might force the issue for Domínguez."

"He'll force the issue for me, too," Wisdom said.

"Are you in command here?"

"That's right."

"Then, Lafe, keep your men where they can't be hit from the other side. If that's Boney's idea, make him come out on the bridge—make him come across the middle of it, to this side—before you respond."

Wisdom clenched his jaw. "I can't ask my men to skulk on American soil, by God! Somebody's deliberately baiting them. They'd have gone across and wiped out that damned dive by now if I'd let them have their way. If one of my men is hit—"

"It will be your fault, Lafe," Hewitt cut in. "I told you, keep them out of sight, out of range—I don't care if you have to pull back to Corpus Christi."

Wisdom hit the table with his fist. "I knew you'd say that. Jeff, the time for diplomacy has passed when they shoot across an international border. I've got snipers stationed where—"

"Where they can start a war with Mexicans because of what one damned renegade American is doing."

"It's the Mexicans' responsibility to police their own territory, clear to the middle of the bridge," Wisdom raged. "That's all we're doing. We'll fire across the line only in retaliation. But we will *not* let anybody fire at us, do you get that? They've been patrolling that town with a full regiment, riding like hell, running people off the streets, making a goddamn circus when they should be keeping the peace. Now you expect American troops to sit here on their hind ends and let somebody take pot-shots into American territory. Like hell!"

So Domínguez had had his telegram, and was not sure

of his own soldiers. When your grip on your men is uncertain, you work them, you ride their tails off, you chouse the civilian population and make them hate your men. Your command then has no friend on earth, nowhere to turn, but you.

Hewitt knew Wisdom's type. He was smart, brave, a gifted commander who earned the loyalty and respect of his men by sharing their dangers and hardships and taking care of them. He blew up easily, like black powder, and made a lot of smoke. But he had sense, too. Hewitt waited until he had run out of breath.

"Lafe," Hewitt said, "do you think I don't know what I'm doing? Do you?"

"I don't know what the hell you're doing and—"

"You're not supposed to know. You've got a job to do. Do it, and let me do mine."

"All right, by God, then don't try to tell me how—"

"Lafe, do you believe that I can wire Washington and, in two hours, have back a reply ordering you to put yourself and your command at my services?"

"Now that's going too far—"

"Do you believe I can do it, though? Do you? Do you? Do you?"

Wisdom locked his hands together, closed his eyes, inflated his cheeks, and blew his breath out noisily. "Oh, dear Lord, and I sold my wife's farm for this life." He moaned and opened his eyes. "Jeff, I think you're bluffing. I don't think you can do anything of the kind, but I'm not going to take chances. You're a damned slippery, conniving, horse-trading pickpocket, and, by God, you're bluffing me and I've got to let you do it."

He gave the captain and the sergeants orders to pull all soldiers back to where they could not see the bridge or be seen from it. They went out into the rain on the double.

"Thank you, Lafe," Hewitt said.

Wisdom felt of his muscles, clenching his jaws again. "You caught me in a good humor, Jeff. That's a hell of a horse. Whoever rode him let him get away with too much, but I'll teach him to tote a soldier. Know what I'm going to call the bullheaded bastard?"

"Hewitt?" said Hewitt.

Wisdom nodded and grinned. They sat in silence for a while. The rain decreased noticeably but did not stop. The thunder and lightning had moved on out over the Gulf, but the record of storms here indicated that this one would be back, with still heavier rains, before morning.

It was almost dark when the door opened and Benito slipped inside. "Sheriff Stern said I'd probably find you here, Mr. Hewitt," he said.

"You're excused, Lafe," said Hewitt. "You don't want to sit in on this."

Wisdom jumped up and went out, grumbling. Benito sat down in the chair he had vacated. The boy was soaked to the skin. He had taken off his boots and put on thong huaraches, to make himself less conspicuous, and he wore an old, tattered shirt.

Hewitt ordered coffee and a ham sandwich for him, and while Benito ate, they put their heads together.

"What do you want to know, Mr. Hewitt?"

"First, Domínguez has got his men out. Can we figure it's because he got a telegram?"

"Oh yes, sure."

"How sure? This is important, Benito."

"I read the telegram."

"*What!*"

"Sure. You could have read it yourself. It came through El Paso and Brownsville. The wires are still down between Matamoros and the south."

That's something I overlooked, Hewitt thought. . . .
"What did it say?"

"It was from the military commandant, in the name of
the President. It told Domínguez to turn over his command to Colonel Gilberto Martínez. And, Mr. Hewitt, it
was to *Colonel* Domínguez, not General Domínguez."

"What about Boney?"

"He is not in la Casa de la Luna Pálida anymore. He
is not anywhere. No one has seen him, and in this rain, a
man must have a roof over him."

"Not if he's a murderous fanatic with a one-track mind.
Did you find out if the rifle is still there?"

"I could not ask about it, but it is no longer hanging
where it used to hang in the kitchen. Mr. Hewitt, there is
something else I heard. Domínguez passed a tax on everybody. They all had to come to the Edifício Municipál and
pay it today. That is where he was when the telegram
came, in a room with a wooden box full of money before
him," said Benito.

"He took the box back with him to his room in the
English warehouse and put it in the safe. He was very
angry, very wild. He will not turn over his soldiers to this
Colonel Martínez, and that is the truth."

"Did you get to talk to any of the troops?"

"Oh, yes."

"How do they feel about him?"

"They hate him but they are afraid." The boy
shrugged. "They are soldiers, Mr. Hewitt. They took an
oath and they will obey him even though they hate him."

"But they do hate him."

"Yes. He had two of them whipped in public yesterday,
and two of them today are chained with a big log across
their shoulders, one at each end. They have to march up
and down in the rain, carrying the log."

Benito tapped Hewitt's arm with the end of his finger. "But they are still Mexican soldiers," he said softly, "and if you meddle in their affairs, you will only drive them to be more loyal to him."

"I won't meddle in their affairs. Benito, there's nothing downriver, below the bridge, is there?"

"Only a few shacks, and when it rains, everybody must move out. It is all under water now."

"How about upriver?"

"Not so bad. Only very poor people live close to the river, you understand. Their goats eat the brush, and they smuggle a little and steal a little. You know how it is."

"If a man were to leave la Casa de la Luna Pálida with a rifle and did not want to be seen, where would he go?"

Benito narrowed his eyes. "I see what you mean."

"Do you know that area?"

"I played there as a boy. My cousins used to live there. They were very poor, and I helped them catch frogs to eat. It is a long time, but I don't think it changes much."

"Can you make a little map for me to memorize, so I can find my way down there?"

Benito thought this over. "No, but I could guide you myself." And when Hewitt began shaking his head, Benito went on, "What else can you do? You can't even get across the bridge alone! If they see you with me, they will think it is only another drunken American looking for girls, because only a drunk would try to cross the bridge today. Together, we can do it."

"What about the Mexican troops?"

"What about the American ones?" Benito countered.

"I promise there'll be no trouble from them. How good are our chances of getting across without being shot down by Mexican soldiers?"

"I know where to wait and watch. You are going there to kill Boney, aren't you?"

"No."

"What then?"

"Talk to him."

"About what?"

"You say Domínguez has his headquarters in an English warehouse—would that be Rexford and Whyte?"

"Yes."

"Does Boney know this?"

"I don't see how he could. He only moved there from the Edifício Municipál today." Benito cocked his head thoughtfully. "You know what, Mr. Hewitt?"

"No, what?"

"I don't think you must talk to this Boney at all. Give me half an hour to tell a friend something, and then I think you and I should be somewhere near the warehouse of Rexford and Whyte."

"No, Benito, I do my own dirty work," Hewitt said slowly. "You stay out of it."

Benito finished his sandwich and wiped his hands carefully on his damp shirt. From his pants pocket he took a handsome brass case about the size of a wallet. He opened it and took out some long Egyptian cigarettes and a few matches.

"When did you start smoking?" said Hewitt.

"I smoke," said Benito, "only when I can afford it."

"I see. Where did you get that outfit?"

Benito lovingly closed the brass case and put it in his pocket. "From General Domínguez," he said, between puffs, "although he did not know it at the time. As I said earlier, Mr. Hewitt—what else can you do?"

"My boy," said Hewitt, "you've got the makings of a hell of a lawyer."

CHAPTER NINETEEN

From the bridge, not a light showed on the American side, and only a few on the Mexican side—far from the river, and very dim. The rain had been a light, steady drizzle for some time. Now it began to beat a little harder.

Hewitt and Benito had the same idea—go while the rain was making noise enough to cover their footsteps. They crouched to reduce their profiles and ran across into Mexican territory. No one challenged them. They stopped for Hewitt to get his bearings on the upstream side of the bridge.

Benito pointed to a squat, tile-roofed building across the wide international street. This, he said, was la Casa de la Luna Pálida. If there was anyone in it, he was keeping himself well hidden.

Benito led the way down a sandy bank below the level of the unpaved street. The footing leveled off suddenly. They groped their way carefully between the clumps of willows. Hewitt began to get a good feeling, a lucky feeling, when the rain suddenly let up. Rain when you needed it, no rain when you didn't—you couldn't beat that combination.

A little, thatched *jacal,* a round shanty with a thatched

roof, loomed ahead of them. A small dog ran out to challenge them. Benito spoke to it. The dog kept on barking. Hewitt could see the edge of a flat-roofed, open porch of some kind on the other side. Benito touched him on the arm.

"Wait here," he whispered.

He disappeared. In a moment he came back, followed by three men, all smoking long Egyptian cigarettes boldly. By their glow, Hewitt thought he could see that the men wore the plain, brown, cotton uniform of infantry *voluntarios*.

Benito presented them ceremoniously and Hewitt shook their hands with equal ceremony. "They told Boney where to find General Domínguez," Benito said in Spanish. "He departed immediately, carrying the rifle. Now they want to know how they can help you."

"Nothing more, thank you," Hewitt said, with a bow to the three.

"We owe it to you to guide you there," said one.

"Why?" said Hewitt. "Benito knows the way. You have wives and children—I have none. A few hours in jail, until Colonel Martínez comes—what is that to me? But your wives and children have wept enough today."

"That you understand that no one is afraid," one growled.

"Who speaks of fear? Only that brave men rest for tomorrow. A million thanks."

Another ceremonious handshake, and Benito turned toward the town, feeling his way along parallel to the international road, the rush of the current of the river receding behind them. More and better buildings began to appear.

And suddenly they could hear, not far away, the shout of loud, angry, military commands. Bit-rings jingled and several horses—at least a dozen, Hewitt thought, by the sound—went jinking off through the darkness on tight reins. Hewitt smiled to himself in the darkness. A display of force to keep troops in line and the population cowed was one thing—to run men and horses to death in the middle of the night when there was no one abroad to see was the idiocy of desperation.

They crossed the road boldly and again no one challenged them. Hewitt knew where he was now. They went down a short street that ran parallel to the river, turned south again at the first muddy intersection, and stopped.

Benito pointed across the street. Hewitt muttered, "Sí, pero donde está Boney?"

"God knows," Benito replied.

Hewitt considered. Across the street, and still two hundred yards away, stood a big, solid building. This was the warehouse of Rexford and Whyte, Ltd., exporters of grain, cotton, live and dressed beef, semiprecious stones and crude gold, hides and leather, and now and then horses. The company imported cloth, olive oil, lamp oil, wheat flour, guns, and ammunition—and now and then horses.

The British mercantile interests survived no matter who was President or how well or badly he governed Mexico. One thing was sure, Hewitt need not let anything that happened to Rexford and Whyte, Ltd., weigh on his conscience.

"This is too long a shot by night for Boney," he said. "He'll be up closer. I don't want to take a chance on being mistaken for Domínguez. Is there a back way into the warehouse?"

"A door with thirty or forty men guarding it," Benito replied. "Otherwise, only windows."

"How close can we approach without being detected?"

"Not very close. I can show you the way."

"Let's go, then."

They crossed the street almost at a run, hitting the deep shadows on the other side just in time. A patrol of a dozen *Lanceros* came the very way they had come, at a hard gallop, turned toward Rexford and Whyte with a right-angle precision that hurled mud at Hewitt and Benito, and pulled up in front of the warehouse. A man in a waterproof cape came out to meet them.

"Nothing to report," said the commander of the detail. "We saw no one on the street. There are no other soldiers."

"Continue your patrol," said the man on the ground.

"But, by God, my men and horses—"

"Continue your patrol," the man on the ground repeated sharply. "That is the general's order. *Viva* Mexico!"

"*Viva* Domínguez," said the detail's officer. He gave an order. His men followed him on up the street at a more sedate pace.

Hewitt and Benito rounded a dark building and found themselves in a narrow alley that seemed to drain all the water that ran off the roofs for blocks. It flowed two inches deep here, and swiftly, but at least there was no mud underfoot, and the rush of the water helped muffle the sound of their steps.

They strode out rapidly. Ahead, they could make out the guard at the back door of the warehouse, huddled miserably in the rain, without any shelter whatsoever. They stopped for a look around at the warehouse corner, less than fifty yards from the guards.

"Here's a window," Hewitt whispered. "Let's see what luck we have forcing it."

The adobe walls were eighteen inches thick, the window boarded up with thick planks. It had been a long time since anyone had made an inspection of security here, however, because Hewitt was able to get his fingers between two of the planks and get a grip on one of them.

It gave with a ripping sound when he pulled. He stopped without relinquishing his grip, and they listened carefully for a moment. No sound. He pulled again, but the plank did not yield.

"Help me up," Benito said.

Hewitt gave him a boost so that he could stand on the windowsill. Benito got his fingers under the plank higher up, and pulled. When Hewitt felt the plank give, he put his strength to it, too.

It came away almost without a sound. Benito let it down to Hewitt, who leaned it against the building. "Wait a moment," Benito said, dropping through the opening into the building itself.

He was back almost immediately.

"It seems to be kegs of black powder and boxes of dynamite stored here, Mr. Hewitt," he whispered. "Will they do you any good?"

"Not without fuses and primers," said Hewitt.

"I don't know if any are here," said Benito, "and you bet I did not strike a light."

"Let me think, let me think!"

The rain had stopped, and if his luck was running high tonight, what did that suggest? A man who could not improvise to take advantage of changing conditions did not deserve to win.

"How heavy are those kegs of powder?"

"About fifty pounds. They'll go through the window without any trouble."

"All right, Benito, let's have all you can hand to me, until I tell you to stop."

Hewitt told him to stop when he had a dozen kegs

stacked on the ground outside the window. He helped Benito out while he felt the kegs in the darkness. They were strong kegs of good British oak, not a defective one in the pile.

"*Ai Dios*, how you handle that stuff," Benito complained. "We shall both be blown to hell, Mr. Hewitt."

Hewitt had found the bung in one by feel, and, also by feel, a small rock about the same size. "What I need now," he said, "is a club, a chunk of wood," he said. "Something that won't make a spark when I hammer with it. This stuff isn't like dynamite. It needs flame or a spark, while dynamite needs shock, percussion."

Benito vanished. He came back carrying a short length of two-by-four. "I hope," he whispered, "that you know what you're doing."

"Bet on it," said Hewitt. "Go watch the guards at the back door. If they hear me, warn me."

He put the rock on the bung of the keg and tapped it with the two-by-four. He felt it begin to give, and, when Benito said nothing, used both hands to pound harder.

The wooden bung went into the powder. He hissed for Benito, who came running. "Follow me," he said, "but don't walk in the stuff. I'm going to lay a train to touch off the whole stack."

"My God, won't that touch off what's left inside?"

Hewitt picked up the keg and tucked it under his arm, bung down, with his hand over the hole. "That," he said, "is what I'm hoping. We've got to get Domínguez out of there."

He let the powder run out in a stream around the stacked kegs. Trailing black powder behind him, he walked slowly up the alley, almost to the street. There the powder ran out. He left Benito to mark the spot and went to the street to reconnoiter.

He came back. "Right around the corner, to the right," he whispered, "is a doorway. This is going to light up and travel like hell. We've got to get into that doorway before those kegs go. Start running!"

He knelt and struck a match. Benito set off like a deer the moment the match glowed. Hewitt dropped it into the powder train and saw the bright, hot flame race across the alley and swarm over the kegs like the tail of a comet. The roar of flame and the stench of smoke followed him as he raced toward the street.

He collided with Benito, who pulled him into the deep-set doorway. It seemed like hours to Hewitt, and he had almost given up, when the flames ate through one of the stacked kegs. It went off with a roar, showering fire twice the height of the warehouse.

Another keg went, and then another. The next one had been blown out into the street before it, too, exploded with a blinding flash and a wave of concussion that rolled like an invisible sea down the street.

The shouts inside the warehouse were almost drowned out by the shuddering rumble of the exploding kegs. One lit on the flat roof of the building and fell off into the street. The flames burned through the oak before it hit the ground, and again there was that blinding fulgor and that hot, hard tide of flowing air.

The whole regimental staff came tumbling out the front door of the warehouse and into the glare. Hewitt thought he was the only man there to hear the crack of the Winchester in all that noise, and he heard it only because he was listening for it. It came from directly across the street. He saw the muzzle flash from what seemed to be the shelter of a low adobe wall, and he heard the scream of a heavy slug driven by a big charge of smokeless powder.

He saw Domínguez go down inertly, the way a man falls when he has been drilled through the brain. Hewitt began running across the street, with Benito behind him. He knew that Boney would wait only to make sure he had hit his man. Then he would get out of there as fast as he could, if he had any sense at all—and when it came to survival, Boney had that kind of sense.

There was enough light from something that was burning in front of the adobe warehouse for him to see the wall from which Boney had fired. He took a chance and jumped it, and went sprawling in the mud beyond. He got out his .45 as he fell, came up to his knees, and crouched there for a second or two.

Boney was fumbling in the dark for a gate, cursing under his breath, a sound that was almost weeping. There was a low tree with a thick trunk near Hewitt. "Stay there and stay low to the ground, Benito," Hewitt snapped. "Just stay out of my way, that's all."

He dashed for the tree, and made it. From behind it he called, "George, this is Hewitt. Do you want to come quietly, or am I going to have to come after you?"

In the street behind him, at the front of the warehouse, there was pandemonium. No one was shooting, but no one had taken command, either. But in front of Hewitt, in the darkness of this little enclosed courtyard, ankle-deep in mud, there was only silence.

But he knew that Boney was there. Something had gone wrong for him, a gate that had been closed after he'd come through—something like that. The explosions had stunned him, too, probably. He had waited to get his shot because that was the kind of man George Boney was, but now all he thought of was getting away and he could not get away.

"Mr. Hewitt," he called shrilly.

"Yes?" Hewitt replied.

"We's both Americans," Boney whimpered. "You cain't shoot me down like a dog, and you cain't let them sojers git hold of me."

"What's your proposition?"

"If I give up peaceful, will you git me back across the river?"

"I'd a lot rather gun you down, you son of a bitch. Why don't you come out shooting?"

"You're a trick shot, Mr. Hewitt, God durn it, and I never did claim to be. Come on, git me out of here afore them sojers catch me."

Hewitt had killed men in his time and had never lost sleep over it. He would repent the death of this one less than most, but even when he called up the picture of Mose Kirk dangling from a rope, he could not make himself shoot Boney down in cold blood.

"All right, George," he said, "hold the rifle over your head in both hands—*both* hands, now!—and walk toward me."

"I cain't even see where you are, Mr. Hewitt."

"Just keep walking toward the wall from where you shot General Domínguez. Don't worry about me—I'll find you when I'm ready."

"You won't just shoot me down, now?"

"No. If you'd rather, you can go for your gun. I don't give a damn how you play it, George."

"I'm comin', I'm comin'!"

In a moment, Hewitt saw the silhouette moving toward him, both hands in sight, clasping the rifle high overhead. He waited until Boney was almost to the wall, and he could hear every taut, trembling breath he drew. He stepped out behind him and jammed the muzzle of his .45 into his back.

Boney moaned and flinched and almost fell to his knees. "Just hold that pose, George," Hewitt said. "Benito, come here and take this rifle."

Benito came over the wall, keeping well away from Boney, and held out his hand. Boney cautiously lowered his left hand, with the rifle in it. Benito took it. Hewitt reached around to lift Boney's .45 out of his holster, and then felt him for other guns. He had none.

"You can put your hands down now, George—behind you, because I'm going to tie your wrists together. That's how we're going back across the bridge."

He took a braided leather rope, limber and strong, from his hip pocket, and with it tied Boney's wrists tightly together. Benito knew how to get them out of this little walled-in courtyard, but just as they started walking down the international road toward the bridge, a file of soldiers came trotting toward them.

Boney moaned and flattened himself against the wall. Hewitt and Benito fell back, too, one on either side of him. There they waited until the soldiers had passed.

"That's a ragged-ass bunch," Benito said, "but those are good horses. They don't look like any of Domínguez's men to me."

"That," said Hewitt, "is Colonel Martínez, coming to take command." He jabbed Boney with the muzzle of his gun. "Let's go, George. We're going to walk fast, now, right down the middle of the bridge, like honest men on honest business. Let's step right along, there."

"Sure, Mr. Hewitt, but I could walk easier with my hands loose. If I trip and fall, what then?"

"You'll get a bruise or two, but nothing like what Mose Kirk got. You've run out of luck, George."

"Now you cain't tell me, Mr. Hewitt, that it's a crime in

the United States, what happened back there at Hangman's Springs. Domínguez, he done that, not me."

"Sure, sure." Hewitt prodded him again. "Step along, George. Hurry!"

"I'm hurryin', Mr. Hewitt, but you got to turn me loose when we reach the American side."

Somewhere up ahead, on American soil, someone was holding some restless horses. The explosions would have been clearly audible and brightly visible from far north of Brownsville. Hewitt had no doubt that Major Lafe Wisdom would send men up to guard the approaches to the bridge. They would be his own cavalrymen, but they would be dismounted and—

"Halt! Who goes there?" came a voice.

"This is Mr. Hewitt, with a friend and a prisoner," Hewitt replied.

"Come forward and be recognized."

He prodded Boney forward to where a hard-faced old sergeant waited, three dismounted troopers behind him. Hewitt took out a cigar and lighted it, to make it easier for the man to recognize him.

"Yes, sir, Mr. Hewitt," the sergeant said, "Major Wisdom will be mighty glad to see you, mighty glad! Who is this jaybird here?"

"This jaybird," said Hewitt, "goes into the custody of Sheriff Stern. This is Jim Barkalow, wanted in Kansas for two murders."

"Aw, no!" Boney quavered. "Aw, no, Mr. Hewitt!"

"Aw, yes, George," Hewitt replied. "Know what that is I tied your wrists together with? That's the rope Mose Kirk was hanged with. Get going, man—and, Benito, you run ahead and tell Bill to get a cell ready. I told you, George, you have run out of luck tonight."

CHAPTER TWENTY

Before he opened his eyes, he knew it was going to be another hot one. Bill Stern's office deputy was being as quiet as he could, but the two prisoners in the cells were quarreling and making the deputy nervous, and he dropped things. Hewitt rolled over and sat up.

"Where are my clothes?" he said.

"Bill sent 'em home for his wife to wash and iron dry. He said to let you sleep all day if you could, but them two been at it all night," the deputy said.

"Well," Hewitt yawned, "they've got plenty to talk about." His watch showed nine forty-five. He ached all over, but it was the healthy ache of weariness well earned. "Where could a man get a cup of coffee?"

"All I've got is this muck, but I kin have breakfast sent over while you wash and shave, and the Lone Star makes good coffee."

"Muck is just what I need now."

The deputy poured a tin cup of rank brew from the pot on the office stove. He showed Hewitt where he could bathe and shave. He sent a boy to the sheriff's house for Hewitt's clothes, and to the Lone Star for breakfast.

Conrad Meuse came in as Hewitt was eating bacon, grits, fried beans, and eggs at the sheriff's desk. "Good morning, Jefferson," he said with what might have been excessive politeness. "It would appear that you have your murderers. Aristide will pay a suitable reward."

Hewitt shook his head and indicated a chair, in which Conrad sat down. Conrad was dressed as formally as ever. If the heat bothered him, his inner discipline did not permit him to show it.

"It's not necessary," said Hewitt. "There's a thousand dollars out on Boney from Kansas."

"I know, but that's not much money."

"Every little bit helps, Conrad. Aristide owes us something for bringing him up here. You made that deal. How much does that come to?"

"Unfortunately," said Conrad, "the deal was to escort him to Corpus Christi."

"We can still do that."

"We?"

"Well, I, then. How much was that deal?"

"Five thousand."

"There you are, Conrad. Six thousand isn't a bad three weeks' pay. We've worked for less. What's happening in Matamoros?"

"Sheriff Stern went over to see for himself. There's a military band playing in the plaza, one hears, and a barbecue and fiesta under way. Colonel Martínez has invited Aristide, but I doubt he'll go."

"Why not?"

"He has had no word from President Díaz, only a wire from the Mexican minister in Washington."

Hewitt grinned. "Aristide has been a bad boy, Conrad. Uncle Porfirio has to uphold the dignity of his office. I would advise Aristide to let his shirttail hang out and eat barbecued beef with the enlisted men, instead of pushing on to Corpus Christi. There are times when every man owes it to his country to come home, and I'd say this is Aristide's last and best chance to be a patriot."

"On Díaz's terms. It's not easy, Jefferson."

"It's much easier than if he were dead. There have been enough senseless deaths."

Hewitt poured himself another cup of coffee. Conrad drummed on the desk with his blunt fingers. "It would be easier," he said, "if he had his diamonds back. They mean more to him than their cash value. They represent pride, security, family continuity. His father started the collection, you know. I believe he would abandon going on to Corpus Christi, return to Mexico, and pay us liberally to take the diamonds to New York for safe storage."

"Oh, yes," Hewitt said thoughtfully, "the diamonds."

"Exactly. Was that another of your bluffs?"

"Oh, by no means!"

"How long will it take you to recover them?"

"That depends on several things. Suppose you and I ride out and have a chat with Aristide as soon as I have eaten. How are Helen and Josefina this morning?"

"Helen is well. She is so grateful that things have turned out well. She does not want her husband to be an exile from his own country. Josefina is ill, I'm afraid. She was unable to eat a bite this morning."

"That's perfectly normal," said Hewitt, "although an old stag like you wouldn't understand."

Again, Conrad played a tattoo on the desk with his fingers. "We must do something about the diamonds."

"We?" Hewitt said, lighting his first cigar of the day.

"Very well, then, you," Conrad said.

Hewitt stood up, and when Conrad stood up too, Hewitt threw an arm across his shoulders. "I don't mean to tease you, old friend, but it's a good thing for you to see some of the problems I encounter in the field. I like the work I do, understand that. I wouldn't trade jobs with you. But sometimes I'm forced to make snap judgments and then recover in my own way, and it's not always easy."

"Perhaps not," Conrad said stiffly, "but it's always expensive, and somehow there's always a woman in the background. Now, when there is one who would make you a suitable wife, the attractive daughter of a rich man who *wants* her to marry you, you are a flighty stag."

"Hardly that," Hewitt said, wincing. "How much would Aristide pay you to take the diamonds to New York? Come on, Conrad—I know you! What's the figure?"

"He would pay *us* ten thousand. Not me, *us*."

"Well, I haven't seen New York in a long time. He'll pay expenses, too, of course? Train fare and first-class hotels?"

It was Conrad's turn to wince. "You are an expensive man to do business with. I don't believe he would argue over expenses if he could put his hands on the Castañeda family diamonds, however."

"Let's go talk to him."

Aristide and his wife were sitting in the shade of the pergola, fanning themselves with fans made from clipped and painted palmetto fronds. Helen greeted Hewitt with a warm smile, but she waited for her husband to set the tone of the meeting, and Aristide was stiffly formal.

"You have had your way, friend Hewitt," he said, "as you meant to from the first."

"That's right," said Hewitt. "You deceived me, Aristide. You led me blindly up to the very door of a revolution. Nobody forces me to take sides that way."

"I will not be forced to knuckle under to Porfirio Díaz, either."

"You don't have to. You have made your offer of friendship and support. Is the presidency of Mexico for sale for a handful of horses? If you were President, would you permit yourself to be blackmailed into a handshake by a man stopped in the act of deserting his country?"

Aristide's swarthy, stony face went white. "What are you trying to say, friend Hewitt?"

"Take your beating. Go over there and offer your hand to Colonel Martínez. Join the fiesta, prove you're one of them. I'll go see Josefina now, while you and Conrad talk it over."

"She won't see you," Aristide said.

Hewitt did not reply. He went in the back door, spoke amiably to the servant who was cutting up chickens in the kitchen, and passed on to the front of the house. The front door was open and there was a light breeze. The bright sunshine, after the oppressive overcast of the past few days, made the little room look cheerful.

Josefina sat in a rocking chair in the corner, doing nothing. Her eyes flicked around when he came into the room, but then went back to staring blindly out the door.

"May I sit down?" Hewitt said.

"Do as you damn please," she replied. "I saw you talking to Father, and let's get one thing straight right now. I wouldn't marry you if you were the last son of a bitch on earth."

Hewitt nodded. "You're a smart girl. That kind of horse-trade marriage isn't for you."

"*What!*"

"Someday you'll meet a man you'll love enough to want to marry, and it would be a shame if you let yourself be pushed into the wrong marriage now, just to give Mose Kirk's baby a name. Hold out for what you really want, Josefina."

She did not move, but he knew she was fighting hard to

keep her tears from showing. "But I don't know what it is I want," she said.

"Oh well, you can wait to find that out. First comes the business of having the baby. That's going to be hard for your father to accept, so I hope you'll be kind to him. Have your way, of course, but be kind."

"Have my way?"

"Of course. You mean to keep the baby, don't you?"

"I'll never give the baby up—never!"

"But do you need to make your father humiliate himself—as he wants President Díaz to humiliate himself? It's easy to be a good loser, Josefina. Be a good winner! Show your father how to do things gallantly, gracefully, with poise and tact and self-confidence."

She put her head in one hand, her elbow on the arm of the rocker, and let herself weep a few sobs. "I know what you mean, Hewitt, you bastard! That's what Helen says, too."

"She has turned out to be a good friend, after all, hasn't she?"

Josefina nodded. "Yes, and I treated her dreadfully for so long! I couldn't stand the thought of her being my father's wife—running his house—having his child—being the señora and making the decisions for the servants—and now she has turned out to be the sweetest, kindest person I have ever known."

"Then why," said Hewitt, "don't you give back the diamonds?"

She moved like a panther, stiffening in the chair and clutching its arms with both hands. Her eyes had gone dry of tears as she stared at him.

"You devil!" she whispered. "How—when—where did you get into my things? Impossible! But how else could you know?"

"Oh, nonsense," he said mildly. "You nipped them a long time ago, didn't you? You took them and left your father and Helen the fakes, to spite both of them. And I'm quite happy that you did. If I had known about them, I wouldn't have made that trip up from the rancho without a military escort. And if we had been robbed, I'm sure you would have bluffed it out some way."

She nodded. "They were in the vase on the left side of the carriage, until after we crossed the river. Then I put them in with my underwear." She closed her eyes to think it over for a moment. He saw her shake her head. She opened her eyes and said, "Hewitt, damn it, I can't do it."

"Let Helen know you felt that way about her, you mean?"

"Yes. How can I get the stones back to him?"

"Let me. Hand them over to me and I'll see that he gets them back."

"How will you explain it, though?"

"Why do I have to explain? I'm Jefferson Hewitt, remember? You have your little mysteries, and I have mine. Go get them. You and I are a lot alike in many ways, my dear. I don't tell everything, either."

She studied him narrowly at some length. "Hewitt, you almost tempt me to marry you."

"But I wouldn't marry you if you were—"

"—the last woman on earth," she finished for him, almost with a smile. "All right, wait here."

She went into her bedroom and came back with a small deerskin pouch, identical to the one that Aristide had produced to exhibit the paste stones. Hewitt did not open it. He dropped it negligently into the pocket of his coat and smiled at her.

"Since we can't be husband and wife," he said, "let's be friends."

She took his hand and returned his firm clasp. "All right," she said, "but you surely must be the most obnoxiously egotistical man on earth."

"That's quite possibly true," he said cheerfully. "Better remain inside and indisposed for a while, my dear. I doubt you're actress enough to keep from betraying yourself. You may make a miraculous recovery when you hear the sounds of jubilation when I return with the diamonds. Give me thirty minutes."

"You enjoy these little acts, don't you?" she said.

"Well," he said, "I try to. Good luck. I think you can be a very attractive, successful, and happy woman, if only you can learn to control that bitchiness."

He went out, untied Coco, and led him to the pergola. The two men were silent and glum, but Helen looked at him expectantly.

"How is she, Mr. Hewitt?"

"Not exactly well, but I'm sure she'll soon be over it. May I look forward to having lunch with you?"

"Of course," she said, "but are you leaving now?"

"Yes. I have an appointment at eleven, in Brownsville. It won't take long."

"Will one o'clock be convenient to you?"

"Quite." He swung up into the saddle. "And then, Aristide, I think you must plan to attend the fiesta. Ride this horse over and present him formally to Colonel Martínez. That's the handsome thing to do, the act of a *caballero*— and even President Díaz won't have so fine a horse!"

Aristide narrowed his eyes thoughtfully, but Conrad scowled. "Why must you leave now, when we have so many unsettled problems?" he said.

"Why," said Hewitt, "to get the diamonds, of course."

He gave Coco his head and let him have the run he G 31 needed. By the time he got back, Conrad would have struck his deal with Aristide, Josefina would have recovered her health, peace of mind, and poise, and the legend of Jefferson Hewitt would have extended still another long notch. In the pocket of his coat, one of the finest collections of unset diamonds in the world bounced lightly. On the whole, it was one of the most beautiful mornings he could remember.

LEE COUNTY LIBRARY
SANFORD, N. C.